THE

OF GOSSIP

Anne -
Happy reading!
Pamela

PAMELA MANN

First published in paperback by
Michael Terence Publishing in 2017
www.mtp.agency

www.pamela-mann.com

ISBN 978-1-520-95263-5

Dedication

To Jean

My irreplaceable friend

"A lie gets half-way around the world before the truth has a chance to get its pants on."

Sir Winston Churchill

THE BIRTH OF GOSSIP

PAMELA MANN

Chapter 1

1562
Hertfordshire, England

Squelching through the mud, the two midwives bent their thin, brown-clad bodies into the wind. Sarah said something. But with her chin tucked into her chest, her words chased along the gale and were lost. Dorothy moved a little closer to her friend.

"What did you say, Sarah? Why're you whispering?"

"I said", she hissed, "That woman's a witch."

"Which woman?"

"You know. Margory Francis or whatever her name is."

"You mean the new midwife?"

"Who else? The one with the big nose, little eyes, lives on her own and has a mole on her arm."

"Well, I think I've got a mole on my..." Dorothy nearly slipped as she tried to point to her back.

"Dorothy, you're not listening. Everybody knows a mole's the devil's mark."

"Well, really..."

"And, she moved here on the 7th of the month."

"Oh all right then. Even I know that's not a good omen. But she hasn't lost a mother or baby since moving here. That's good, not bad, isn't it?"

"Magic water."

"What? Speak up, Sarah. Only the wind can hear."

"She uses magic water in the deliveries."

"How can water be magic?"

"Well, I don't know, do I, but it must be why she hasn't had any deaths."

"Right. Well. You and I've been delivering babies here for years and the village water's always been good enough for us, hasn't it."

"Exactly."

"I just ignore the bits of – er, you know - excrement. You do, too, Sarah, don't you?"

"'Course. I'm not going to let some waddling duck of a woman come between me and my earnings. This old, woollen dress is all I've got now. Look at its hem. Covered in mud. We've got to start spreading the word, Sarah – and quick. There's something suspicious about Mistress Margory Francis, and we're going to find out what it is. Shhh. Here she comes now."

Chapter 2

It had been raining for days. And now there was also lashing wind. Toiling through the mud, I dragged my weary weight up Brockminster's steep street, struggling for breath. For once, other thoughts were competing with my desire for sweetmeats - The Manor and Hugh Taylor. I couldn't thank Lord Winchester enough for his suggestion of putting Hugh in charge of my estate. He certainly seemed a very capable man, and I was looking forward to getting to know him better. But I was still married to Arthur; that was something the Brockminster villagers mustn't know. It meant I had to stop thinking about how I felt when looking at Hugh's face. It wasn't handsome, but it was an open, honest face, framed by dark brown curls, one of which always seemed to escape from his hat. And those shoulders. So broad I felt they could support any worries I may have as well as his own. It was strange really. I had always been attracted to very tall, handsome men, like Arthur, and Hugh was neither tall nor good looking. He was just, well, a kind, thoughtful man. But why was I allowing my thoughts to wander like this? After all, he wouldn't be interested in plain, overweight me. Would he? Oh dear, I really must try and avoid the baker's.

People hurrying to church jostled me from my thoughts. How long had someone been tugging at my skirt? Now they were shouting something. I ignored them. I'd so little money of my own now that, much as I would like to, I couldn't give any of it to beggars. There were so many of them! Without turning, I tried to shake off the hand, but still it clung.

"Please let go of my skirts. I haven't any money to give you."

"I don't want your money. You're a midwife, aren't...?"

In spite of the passing chatter, I realised then that the voice was a woman's. But her pleadings were suddenly cut short by her piercing shriek. Turning, I saw that her chemise was wet, her face contorted in pain - she was clearly in the throes of labour! I stopped and drew breath. This stranger needed me. I had the usual surge of delight, knowing that I could work with her in producing a healthy baby. Although I'd done it so many times I'd lost count, I never failed to experience a depth of emotion that couldn't be contained in the deepest of wells. I had had many successful deliveries, but each birth was different. For me, the moment of utmost pleasure was placing the precious bundle into the arms of its relieved mother. If only I had had a child. Even one would have been wonderful. But I put those thoughts aside. I must help this woman who was lucky enough to be experiencing one of the world's wonders. Now feeling perfectly calm, I asked,

"What's your name?"

"Abigail." Then, turning to the passers-by, I told them,

"Help me get Abigail into the church. Yes, I know a service will have just started, but she's in labour and it's the closest place that's at all suitable. Hurry!

Chapter 3

Making use of this Protestant church suited my secret well. As we pushed open the great doors, the congregation turned, the singing dwindling. The Minister was quick to join me in taking charge as far as was appropriate. I knew that he and his wife had several children, so he wasn't a stranger to childbirth, and showed this knowledge in saying,

"Clear an area in The Lady Chapel so that this woman has somewhere to lie down. Gentlemen of the group, you will want to leave, and any of you ladies who can be of help, please stay. The friends and neighbours the lady has already invited won't be able to come, unfortunately, so we shall rely on you to give her comfort and encouragement. I shall take my leave, also."

Seeing a young boy with his mother, I went over to them.

"Could your son run as fast as he can to get my bag? I live in a cottage on Lord Winchester's estate. If he brings it back quickly, he'll be rewarded."

At the sound of a reward, the boy's little legs began to spin. He was soon to return with my black bag of grease, scissors (which I was delighted to have acquired as they were rare), needle and thread, as well as my precious water. When I pressed a 3 pence piece into his small hand, he looked at me with shining eyes as his mother led him away.

"Thanks ever so, miss."

As I was withdrawing the water from my bag, a woman standing nearby asked,

"What's that?"

"I keep a supply of boiled water in my bag to wash my hands and the newborn babe."

"Why do you use boiled water?"

"I always have, as did my mother. It was she who told me that all sorts of diseases can be carried by water. Also, it doesn't seem right to risk using unclean water to welcome new, pure life into the world. I've never lost a mother or baby and, although I don't know why that is, it may be because I use clean water."

At that, I heard whispers and, glancing around, saw a small group of young girls, one of whose faces seemed familiar. Wasn't she the maid from Brockminster Hall? As her hand was over her mouth, I couldn't be sure, but I could hear a little of what she was saying,

"Maybe it's the magic water we've heard about. This woman isn't any more skilled than our two village midwives. They're saying she uses other powers, just like witches do. You'd think she'd use some of that water to change her face, wouldn't you?"

The girls were doubled over, giggling. My expertise had never been questioned before, so this silly chatter puzzled me. However, I certainly didn't intend to let a few young girls distract me from my work here.

"If you girls want to help, I'll show you what to do. If you don't, then leave. There's important work to be done here."

They scuttled out, still laughing and muttering, "Don't know why she wants anybody's help when she uses magic water. Wonder what Sarah's going to say? She won't be earning any money from this delivery."

Abigail's contractions were now speeding up, so I

needed to fully focus on helping her,

"If anyone else would rather chatter than support Abigail, I suggest you also leave now."

The ladies quickly stopped talking and looked at me expectantly. I smiled,

"Thank you. You two ladies, mop her brow, you four, support her shoulders and upper body when she wants to move position, two of you please comfort her. You can leave the rest to me. I've never had any deaths of either babies or mothers, and I don't intend to start now."

"Help me! Help me!"

Abigail's frightened eyes penetrated mine, her screams piercing the air like lightning. Her hands clutched her helpers', turning them white.

As though from far away, I heard one of the women say,

"Thank goodness this midwife knows what she's doing. How can she stay so calm? Did you see how she was constantly keeping everything clean with that water she uses?"

Poor Abigail's shrieks reached the rafters for several hours, until, eventually, they were matched by lusty yells. Everyone sighed with relief as the healthy boy baby was born, and, after cutting the cord, I placed him tenderly into his exhausted mother's arms.

"You have a beautiful baby boy", I told her. I felt my eyes glaze with tears as I gazed into his wrinkled little face. How I longed for a baby of my own to love. Looking up at me, Abigail smiled weakly.

"Thank you".

Suddenly the church door's loud thud made everyone jump as it flew open and hit the wall. Fury stood there, arms akimbo.

"What's this I hear about you stealing my patient? Why did you deal with the delivery? Everyone knows that I'm Abigail's midwife."

Opening my mouth to reply, one of the women stepped forward, looking at me admiringly.

"Sarah. Mistress Francis did an excellent job under very difficult circumstances. Abigail needed help fast and that's what she got. Fast, expert help."

Turning away, the woman muttered to the others,

"And she kept the mother and baby alive, which is more than you might have done."

Muffled agreement and nodding of heads greeted these softly spoken words.

At that, Sarah screwed up her stony face, turned and left, slamming the door behind her.

The woman looked at me.

"A warning. That won't be the last you'll hear of this."

Chapter 4

My move to Brockminster from Greenwillows had been fortuitous. The Manor, my beloved home since birth, had changed, and part of that difference was the visitors. My husband, Arthur, had been right. We now had none. The local gentry had not been seen since my parents were put to the stake; perhaps they didn't want their noses to risk smelling that burning flesh and cascading fat in case they, too, were contaminated.

It was those noses I noticed on my visits to market. And I wasn't the only one.

"Mistress Margory. Wasn't that Sir John, your late father's friend? I'm sure he saw you, then turned away."

Although rather tactless, my servant's observation was not unusual. I was gradually steeling my feelings to accept the gentry's eyes looking, recognising, then turning away, their noses high in the air. I had never liked some of those pompous olfactory appendages anyway. So, if I saw any of them in Greenwillows, I would note whether they had seen me and then, when they obviously had, I would continue to look as they turned away. Had I noticed even a glimmer of a smile, I would have returned it gladly, but that was not to be. Although hurt by this behaviour, I kept these feelings to myself, trying to convince myself that I cared not. But that changed one day.

"Why Mistress Margory, is that you?"

The deeply melodic male voice, with its aristocratic tone, caught me so unawares that I dropped the fresh vegetables I was helping the servants to carry to market.

"Oh, my dear, I'm so sorry. Allow my manservant to help. It is you, Margory, isn't it?"

Seeing me so addressed by this well known Lord, the passing gentry stopped, their mouths cracking into smiles, their eyes showing surprise at my being spoken to in such a friendly way by such a person. As I turned to this gentleman, I suddenly felt very conspicuous in my shabby clothes. It wasn't surprising that he wasn't sure it was me.

"It is indeed I, Lord Winchester, and how well you look."

"Thank you – as do you. It has been some time since I had the pleasure of taking tea with your parents. Bless their souls."

At his kind mention of my parents, tears threatened to well, but I swallowed them into retreat.

"Under normal circumstances, Lord Winchester, I should be more than happy to repeat that invitation. However, it is with regret that I cannot. These are trying times for my household and I would not wish you to see for yourself how they have affected The Manor."

"My dear girl, my own regret is that Lady Winchester and I have not invited you to Brockminster Hall before now. I shall rectify that immediately. My chief groom, Abner, will call with an invitation and I shall not take no for an answer. I insist on knowing what has taken place since the very sad demise of your parents. You will hear from me directly. We do, in any case, also have a request to make."

By the end of this charmingly generous speech - the last statement of which had left me a little puzzled -

I thought the whole county must have gathered, as all I could see was a sea of faces looking down at me amiably. So, drawing myself up to my full five feet and ensuring that I did not, once again, drop the carrots, cabbages and onions at their feet, I smiled graciously. They would not see how deeply affected I had been by Lord Winchester's words.

"Excuse me. Let me pass, please. I must prepare to visit his lordship."

I ignored the raised eyebrows. I was not a toy to be played with when those of the county who considered themselves the great and the good were disposed to take off one, sour mask, and replace it with another, more cordial. This was not Venice, Italy, but Hertfordshire, England.

Chapter 5

The following week, I arose particularly early. It would take several hours to put together the collection of pieces that comprised the gown I would wear for my visit to Brockminster Hall. And these days, I was unused to it. My maid, Ruth, was helping me to get ready and she could barely contain herself.

"Oh, Mistress Margory, it's so exciting! A visit to Lord Winchester! Imagine! And him such a very nice Gentleman and so grand. I remember him making more than one visit to your parents and thinking then how kind he was."

"I agree, Ruth. I am indeed fortunate that mother and father regarded him as one of their dearest friends. I know they would be very happy that he approached me as he did and offered his invitation, although I have no idea what they are going to ask me. Oh dear, can you push me in at the back while I hold my breath? It's been so long since I squeezed into these clothes and now there's even more of me! Whenever I worry, I find a cake has such a calming effect. I really must try to resist them."

Looking at the dresses Ruth had laid out for me, I realised that I had almost forgotten how very beautiful they were. I'd thought that I wouldn't be wearing them again, so which should I choose? The red silk? The purple satin? No, it would be more appropriate for me to wear the demure, fashionable white so favoured by our Queen Elizabeth.

Father had bought this very pretty French gown

for me a few months before his death, which was another reason for me to wear it in the presence of his good friend.

"Lord Winchester is sending his Chief Groom who'll be arriving shortly, so now I need your help getting into the corset, Ruth. These gowns may be beautiful, but they are not as comfortable as the loose robes I wear now. Make it a little tighter, I think, just tight enough that I can breathe. Yes, that's good. Quickly! Help me into the farthingale, overskirt, bodice and sleeves, not forgetting the silk stockings. Oh goodness, are those the horses I hear? I can barely move!"

But move I did and, walking out, a warm feeling ran through me, raising the hairs on my arms, as I saw that all the servants, unbidden, were standing outside the great door to wish me farewell. How lucky I was to have discovered their friendship during these difficult times.

The ride down the dry, dusty Roman road towards Brockminster and London was exhilarating. As we arrived at the Hall and were met by the butler, I thanked Abner, who doffed his hat and smiled. I found it interesting that Lord and Lady Winchester's fine, amiable characters were reflected throughout their household, just as my own parents' goodness had also been stamped upon our servants. With one exception.

Just as the butler was taking my hat and coat, Lord Winchester appeared and strode towards us, acknowledging my curtsy.

"Thank you, Nicholas. I shall take Mistress

Margory into the withdrawing room myself."

With that, he took my arm and we walked into a room with a Venetian ceiling and rich wood panelling on the walls. It was so beautiful that I could barely drag my eyes to the cream brocade sofa on which Lady Winchester was seated; she turned as we entered and Lord Winchester said,

"My dear, you remember Margory, the daughter of my good friend, John, who, together with his wife, Alice, were taken from us."

"Of course. I'm pleased to see you again, Margory, and so very sorry about the passing of your parents. These are, indeed, extremely troubled times. It's very sad indeed that good people such as John and Alice were treated in the way they were."

Then, in an attempt, I think, to stem my tears that she must have noticed glistening, she patted the sofa,

"Come and sit by my side and tell me how you are. My husband told me that he had seen you on market day in Greenwillows and I was so glad. Do have one of the fruit tarts or iced cakes. They don't stay fresh very long, so it would please me to see you enjoy as many as you wish."

It had been some time since I'd indulged my love of such enticing sweetmeats and I closed my eyes as the honeyed taste touched my tongue. How easy it was to forget to take the lady-like bites my mother had instilled. The tasty treats were almost making me forget my curiosity about why I'd been invited here. But Lady Winchester was speaking again,

"I was particularly happy that my husband

happened to see you because we had, in fact, been discussing the possibility of asking if we could call on you in the near future."

At that, I choked a little on the sweet crumbs, responding a little impetuously,

"Oh, Lady Winchester, I do hope you will forgive me when I say that I'm pleased that you did not. The Manor is not the pretty estate it was when my parents were alive. I wonder whether you are aware that I now have little money and am also without a husband. However, the servants and tenants have been kindness itself and are a great source of comfort and help to me."

"Indeed. I do congratulate you on continuing to run the estate under very difficult circumstances. We shall say no more about your husband, and that will remain between us; no one in the village needs to know. We invited you here, my dear, because it may be that we can help. We know that you gained excellent midwifery experience, first alongside your dear, late mother, before going on to deliver babies on your own and becoming a licensed midwife.

Although this is not yet common knowledge, I'm delighted to say that I now require a midwife. As this will be our first child, I'm particularly concerned, naturally, that I am in expert hands such as yours. Also, should all go well, I would want to continue with the same midwife for future children we may be fortunate enough to have. Would you be happy to fulfil those duties for me?"

My heart was beating so fast at this good fortune, I thought Lord and Lady Winchester must hear it. Giving my smiling response, I said,

"I would be greatly honoured, your Ladyship, to help in any way I can. And, indeed, I'd thought that I must seek midwifery work in Brockminster as well as continuing my work in Greenwillows. Thank you."

Then, my feelings of gratitude began to turn to the practical.

"I do have a concern, though."

"What is that, my dear?" Lord and Lady Winchester spoke together.

"When my financial circumstances changed, all our horses had to be sold. That means that, while I'm happy to walk the eight miles from Greenwillows to Brockminster, it would take some considerable time and, when your pains begin, you would need me to be nearby quickly."

At that, his Lordship nodded and seated himself opposite us, while her Ladyship's slight look of concern cleared, I noticed. Lord Winchester said,

"I'm pleased, my dear, that you have raised this subject, as our discussions have also included the question of where you would live, and we have a suggestion for you to consider. We would be delighted if you would accept a cottage on our estate, for which we would not want to accept rent while my wife requires your services. I would also instruct our Estate Manager's subordinate to move to The Manor – with your permission, of course – in order to take charge of your estate, until such time as our child has been delivered. Additionally, you would have access to our stable of horses any time you would like to return to The Manor yourself to ensure that everything is as you wish and that your servants are happy and comfortable."

I must have appeared rather dazed by these proposals and the extreme generosity of Lord and Lady Winchester as, for a moment, I was unable to speak. Lord Winchester broke the silence by addressing his wife,

"My dear, I think that our suggestions have quite surprised Margory. What we don't want is for you to agree to anything that will inconvenience you in any way. What I suggest is that you think about it and, at a time that suits you, I shall come to The Manor with our Deputy Estate Manager, whose name is Hugh Taylor, whom my wife has mentioned. In that way, you can speak to him yourself, show him the house and land and introduce him to your servants and tenants. Remember that this would not be a permanent arrangement, but one to facilitate your being able to help my wife as much as possible during this, her first time. However, these are only our suggestions for you to consider."

Recovering from this unexpected, wonderful offer, I said,

"Your kind, generous plan took me so by surprise that I'm afraid I've been a little impolite. I would be more than happy to help Lady Winchester and am, indeed, honoured that you have thought to enlist my services."

Lady Winchester looked relieved and pleased and said,

"Good. Then my husband and Hugh will visit you on a day and at a time that is convenient. I'm delighted to see you again, Margory, and shall look forward very much to your helping me."

Then, ringing the servants' bell,

"Jane. Mistress Francis is leaving us. Would you wrap the remainder of these sweetmeats so that she may take them with her, then summon Abner to say that she is ready to leave."

The maid had appeared very quickly, almost as though she was nearby, I thought, with an inward smile.

With a curtsey and "Yes, your Ladyship", she left equally rapidly, with a fleeting glance in my direction, I noticed.

Lord Winchester was addressing me,

"I shall look forward to seeing you next week, Margory, when I sincerely hope that all our arrangements can be finalised. We can then decide when you will be taking up residence in what I think is one of our more comfortable tenant cottages."

"You are both very thoughtful and I cannot thank you enough."

Chapter 6

My dear servants had been anxious to hear what had been said at Brockminster Hall and I wasted no time in gathering them together in the great hall to relay all that had happened. My housekeeper, Goodwife Sykes, had been the first to speak.

"I'm sure that I speak for everyone, Mistress Margory, in saying that we shall miss your daily presence at The Manor. However, if you're satisfied with the gentleman you mention and Lord Winchester knows that he will be able to fulfil the duties of estate manager capably, then we shall all be very happy to work to his orders. It is, after all, only a temporary arrangement until her Ladyship has given birth, at which time we shall welcome you back here joyfully."

My next action had been so spontaneous that it required no thought. I stepped forward and gave Goodwife Sykes such a big hug that everyone clapped, and her smile seemed to reach from ear to ear. Suddenly, I felt that perhaps my life and the lives of my servants were beginning to improve, and I'd not felt that for a very long time. Mother and father would have been proud of me, I was sure. For the next week, I, in turn, was particularly pleased with all my servants. They cleaned and polished every room in The Manor, from the great hall to the library and the private suites, so that it gleamed wherever one walked. Even the rush dips and candles were replenished.

The following week, when our visitors' horses were heard, everyone was very excited. They had all ensured that, not only did The Manor look its best, but their clothes had been washed and pressed thoroughly. Nothing could have looked better.

Again, with the servants outside to welcome our visitors, I led Lord Winchester and Hugh Taylor into my favourite withdrawing room, to which were brought the best cakes cook could produce – including gingerbread and my favourite simnel cake, as well as ale. Not one bottle of wine had been left when The Manor was stripped by the soldiers who had taken away my parents.

Generous as always, Lord Winchester had commented,

"My dear Margory, you have treated us very well indeed. The Manor looks magnificent and, what it lacks in silver, it more than makes up for in sparkle and cleanliness. And how wonderful it smells – that Christmas pudding smell of cloves, the freshness of mint and – yes – is that the musky scent of rose petals? I shall be very content to remain here while you get to know Hugh a little, although I can assure you that he is extremely diligent, capable and hard-working; I know he will serve you well."

"With such a commendation, Lord Winchester, I don't need to speak to Master Taylor privately. Let us all take a walk through the estate so that you may see some of our 200 acres for yourselves, as well as meeting a few tenants whose babies I have delivered. Part of our land is demesne but mainly tenant; it also has fisheries which, on special occasions, father would agree to be fished by our tenants. However, I'm sorry to say that the man I called husband – about whom I would prefer not to speak and whose existence is unknown in Brockminster, of course – left the land and its buildings poorly tended. When you have had an opportunity to look further at the estate, Master Taylor, I shall be happy to discuss any changes you think should be made. In the meantime, I've spoken to each and every one of the workers and tenants and they are all content, indeed happy, to welcome a member of your own distinguished household."

I could not have wished this encounter to have gone better. Lord Winchester's reputation of being a very fair, just and generous employer was evident in Hugh Taylor who was as charming as he was congenial. I had no hesitation in leaving my entire estate in this man's hands and was happy to do so immediately. When we returned to The Manor to discuss the final arrangements, I had told Lord Winchester of my decision; he looked both a little surprised and relieved.

"Those are the words I was hoping to hear you say, Margory. I've never had any doubt, of course, as to Hugh's expertise and trustworthiness, but it was necessary for you to reach the same conclusion. I'm delighted that you have done so. Not only that; any anxiety I may have had about my wife's welfare during this first experience of carrying a child is swept away by the knowledge that she is about to be cared for by your qualified and experienced hands. In addition to what we already knew about your midwifery experience from your mother, speaking to your tenants and seeing their healthy children for myself leaves me in no doubt as to your skill. That fact makes me very relieved indeed. It now leaves me free and without anxiety to pursue my own duties, many of which are in London. This means that I'm away quite often and not in a position to check that Lady Katherine is receiving the care and attention I would wish. I shall now be able to make those journeys, safe in the knowledge that she's well cared for – and for that I thank you most sincerely. Of course, you will be well rewarded, once the birth has taken place, and that is something you and I shall talk about when you have moved into the cottage. We shall also need to discuss any other plans you may have while living in Brockminster, as the care of my wife will not require all your time. My only concern is that the two roomed cottage I've put at your disposal may be a difficult adjustment as you have been used to this grand manor house all your life. However, my labourers have been instructed to make it as comfortable as possible and I hope that will suffice. It will, of course, have a bed, table, bench and a stool as well as a cauldron and other cooking utensils – I'm not familiar with these sorts of things, of course. However, I mention it because, once you have taken up residence, you may wish to bring some of your own household goods from The Manor. At the moment, I suggest you wait to see what you may need."

I sighed with pleasure. I cared not at all about the size of the cottage or its contents. Indeed, I was fortunate that it would have more than one room. What was wonderful was having made contact again with such good friends of my parents and being given the flattering opportunity of taking care of Lady Winchester. Just that birth alone would be very helpful financially. Also, while she would be my main responsibility in Brockminster, I would certainly be able to increase my list of patients there. In fact, that had happened sooner than I thought, as the delivery of Abigail's baby had gone very well. The midwife, Sarah's reaction, however, was a warning that I needed to heed. But it had left me a little perplexed as I had made it clear to Abigail that she would be returning to Sarah's care. Where was my blame?

Chapter 7

This was the first time I had ever moved out of The Manor, and it felt very strange. Loneliness had never knocked at my door before. However, I was sure I would quickly make new friends here in Brockminster. I hoped so.

Lady Winchester's servants couldn't have been more helpful, but I did miss my own, whom I had known for many years, some all my life. I kept telling myself that they weren't far away and I would be seeing them as often as possible. I must also begin to look after my own needs, and that wouldn't be easy either. But I would do it. I was determined to do it. I would also do as Lord Winchester had suggested and bring some of the household items from The Manor, once I had settled in. It would be helpful to have familiar belongings around me.

A schedule had been drawn up by Lord and Lady Winchester showing when he expected to be in London, my visits to Lady Winchester – starting once every two weeks and increasing as her time drew closer – and my visits to The Manor, for which a fine horse was loaned to me. This left the rest of the time for me to gain other patients. Again, Lady Winchester had been generosity itself in informing her tenants of my presence. She had pointed out that, as I would be living among them, I would be available to help, when needed. When I asked who had been responsible before for the tenants' births, Lady Winchester had waved my question aside, saying that she had not been happy with the services of the other village midwives. I had wondered why, little knowing that my first meeting with Sarah would be so laced with hostility.

At the time, I'd thought this was an excellent beginning for my ministrations to the would-be mothers on the Brockminster Hall estate and I did not underestimate the helpfulness of Lady Winchester's offer. Also, I needed to ensure that I didn't forget my own tenants' births at The Manor. So, a week after I had moved to Brockminster, I returned there. I was delighted, even in that short space of time, to see that everything was becoming organised once more, particularly on the estate itself. I had sent word ahead that I would like to speak to Hugh and, to my great pleasure, he was there to greet me. My eyes glistened with tears when I took in how well everything and everyone looked. And, when Hugh took my waist to help me down from the horse, I found myself looking into one of the kindest faces I had ever encountered. I lowered my eyes, pretending to smooth the creases from my dress, but could not prevent a blush from spreading. I swallowed and looked at him. I must not allow myself to make the same impetuous mistake I had with Arthur. But when I glanced shyly at him once again, I could see clearly that this man appeared to be entirely different from any I had met before. Walking towards The Manor, I told him,

"I can see already that my home is in very capable hands and I shan't need to concern myself with its welfare."

"Certainly, that is my aim Mistress. However, I do

hope that you'll continue to visit The Manor often, as I know the servants and tenants would like to see you, as would I."

I didn't look at him as he spoke, as I felt I mustn't read too much into his words. After all, this was a business arrangement and I still regarded myself as being a married woman.

"Indeed, Hugh – and do address me as Margory, please – I have drawn up a schedule with Lord and Lady Winchester, setting out my visits to both her Ladyship and The Manor. Shall we go to the library to discuss how these visits will be conducted?"

"Of course. I would like you to know, too, that, should you need to discuss anything concerning The Manor, I am perfectly happy to visit you in Brockminster, if that would be more convenient for you. For me, it would be a pleasure, Margory, to see you more often."

Again, I wasn't sure whether his words, uttered so gently, were simply of a practical nature, or more personal. I shook my emotional feathers. Why would this kind man be interested in a plain peahen like me? Not looking at him, I said briskly,

"Thank you very much indeed. That may be very helpful sometimes. Now, let us take tea, after which I would very much like to speak to Goodwife Sykes, in your presence, of course, and then we shall visit the tenants. I am particularly wanting to see how my would-be mothers are getting on."

Was that a trace of disappointment I saw captured in his eyes?

Chapter 8

Back in Brockminster, and returning Lord Winchester's horse to the stables, I saw Abner, the Chief Groom, whom I had by then met on several occasions. At the outset, he had told me of his wife, Marion's, imminent birth and her difficulty in deciding who would supervise her delivery. He had asked if I would meet her and we had immediately liked each other. She was exactly the sort of friend I needed in my new environment. Where I was rather naive, she was realistic and we had gradually formed a strong bond that was deepened when I delivered her son, Jacob. He was a lusty, lively baby in whom both Marion and I took great pride. Abner immediately walked over to me,

"Good day, Mistress Margory, I hope you're as well as our beautiful baby boy, Jacob. Excellent job you did there."

"Thank you, Abner. I'm certainly well but haven't the energy of your son! I'm just going to see him and Marion. How is she at the moment?"

"Doesn't seem any better, sorry to say. In spite of Lord Winchester's generous suggestion of his own surgeon seeing her, he's totally perplexed, too."

I felt sorry for Abner as well as Marion. They had a close relationship and, as he looked down and scraped his boot in the dried mud, I saw a shadow come over his face. He was clearly worried.

"I'm really sorry to hear that, Abner. I'll make sure I don't stay long as I don't want to tire her."

"Don't you worry about that, Mistress Margory.

She enjoys your company."

Arriving at their small home, Marion had offered me a small ale before taking me to look at Jacob. He was fast asleep, his head turned to one side, his long, dark lashes brushing his perfect skin.

"He's even more beautiful, Marion. Let's not disturb him as I'd like your opinion on something that happened when I delivered another child."

After describing the delivery in the church, I told Marion about Sarah's sudden appearance and how angry she was.

"Why was she annoyed?"

"She said that Abigail was her patient and I'd stolen her. However, just as I was about to reply, one of the women who had helped said very kind words about my work to Sarah. As she certainly didn't want to hear what a good job I'd done, too, she left as abruptly as she'd arrived."

"I'm very sorry to hear that, Margory. You certainly don't want to make enemies of the two other midwives, Sarah and Dorothy. Together with Jane, the maid at Brockminster Hall and Rose, the innkeeper's daughter, they are the worst malicious chatterers in the village. Oh, of course, we all have a few words to say about somebody or other in the village sometimes, but it's rarely spiteful. But there seems to be a growing tendency these days to edge conversation with venom, which never used to happen. What we have to keep in mind is that they must be very envious of your continuous success. It's a level of achievement Sarah and Dorothy have never reached. They've lost both mothers and babies over the years and, while some losses are to be expected, unfortunately, they shouldn't have lost as many as they have. Not only that, some of their newborns have been injured badly during deliveries. Until you came to Brockminster, the villagers accepted these deaths and injuries as being normal, but now they're wondering why you don't have them, too. I've even heard some say it's due to the water you use having special powers. Of course, when I hear any of this nasty nonsense, I try and do something about it. But I'm not always there, of course, to speak up for you, Margory, so you do need to be careful."

I knitted my brows. This was worrying. Marion was the second person that day to warn me, so I knew I must keep this in mind. I listened particularly closely to what she had to say because she was becoming a good friend. She also knew the villagers much better than I did so I knew I must exercise caution.

"Thank you, Marion, for your words of warning. I must admit that I've been enjoying the success of my work so much that I hadn't realised that the other two midwives hadn't been equally successful. However, now I think about it, Lady Winchester did refer to it a little, although very politely."

"That's another cause of their frustration, Margory. Sarah and Dorothy have lived here all their lives and practised midwifery in the village for a long time. Then you, an outsider, from another village, are given the privilege of caring for Lord and Lady Winchester's first-born delivery. Not only that, a cottage has been prepared for you on their own estate and you're asked to tend to the deliveries of the tenants, too. All this is not only lost income for them, but, in their eyes, lost respect, too."

These were all sobering thoughts indeed. How could I have been so blind? I had been so involved in my own troubles at The Manor, that I hadn't considered any of this.

"Thank you, Marion. I shall heed your words and try not to anger them further. But I think that may be easier said than done. I won't, after all, be lowering my standards of midwifery, but I shall try to exercise caution when our paths cross. I'd actually hoped to gain the friendship of Sarah and Dorothy, but, at the moment, that doesn't look very likely. Anyway, it's growing dark and I must return to the cottage. Take good care of yourself, Marion. I'm delighted to see Jacob looking so very well. Oh, it sounds as though he's waking."

I went over to her beautiful bundle who was kicking his plump little legs and looking expectantly at me.

"I can see that he's growing bigger by the day."

I picked him up, much to his delight.

"Oh, he's wonderfully well and very demanding. He's adorable, thanks to your perfect delivery."

"Well, I love my work. Who wouldn't feel a deep pleasure in helping to bring new, wonderful life into God's world while keeping the mother safe, too?"

Chapter 9

Nearing my cottage, I saw what looked to be a piece of black fur that someone had dropped. However, on getting closer, I saw that it was a tiny, black kitten, sitting shivering. It mewed quietly, its soft, pool eyes looking up at me pleadingly. Where had it come from and who did it belong to? I couldn't leave the poor thing outside. It was now so cold the Thames had frozen over again, some saying that Queen Elizabeth herself had been seen walking on the thickly iced river. When I picked it up, it meowed plaintively as though it was thanking me; it was just a tiny bag of bones. Taking it inside, I gave it some water and, from the speed of its little pink tongue lapping, it had obviously not had a drink for some time, so perhaps it hadn't eaten either. As soon as I'd replenished the twigs on the fire, it curled up and promptly fell asleep. I asked some of my neighbours the following morning, but no one seemed to know anything about it, so he became mine. I called him Precious, and that's what he was to me until the day he died so violently.

Chapter 10

That morning, as I was taking a closer look at my small patch of garden to see what was growing there, one of the tenants came rushing up,

"Agnes Fielding has gone into labour and needs a midwife right away. Lady Winchester tells me that you'll be dealing with the tenants' births now, so you'd better come quick. I've told the friends and neighbours she wanted to be there to go in right away."

Grabbing my black bag, I followed her and went into the small cottage where Agnes was having contractions in fairly fast succession. Most of the women were already doing a good job of supporting her, but I immediately took charge,

"You with the dark hair – sorry, I don't know everybody's name yet – support her shoulders. You, get more towels. This is going to be a short delivery. I can see the head already. Yes, Agnes, push when I say so and not until then. You're doing very well indeed."

With a final shriek-type moan from Agnes, the tiny baby burst into the world with a loud bellow that belied its size.

"Well done, Agnes, You've got a beautiful little girl." I placed the newborn on her mother's chest.

"You should try and sleep now."

"Thank you, but please don't go yet. Would you make my husband's meal? There's no meat so he'll need a lot of grain, water and vegetables. He had to get his own bread, cheese and onions earlier and he'll be hungry when he gets in from the farm."

"Of course, I'll do that now. But when I've done that, I'm sorry but I'll have to go. I'm very tired and two other mothers are nearing full term."

"Oh, can't you stay a while, I was hoping to get to know you a little? I'm really tired but would like the company. The other midwives have always said they're friends as well as healers. I know they sometimes lose newborns and even mothers, but it's nice to have their friendship."

"I'm sure it is, Agnes, and I look forward to you and I becoming friends, too. For now, though, I'll ask your friend to stay with you and if she's worried about anything, I'll tell her to come and get me. But everything's fine, so I'm sure there won't be any problems."

I could tell that Agnes wanted me to stay but I was exhausted. I also needed to ride to The Manor to give thanks in our private place of worship for yet another healthy baby and mother. But that must remain yet another of my secrets. Father was right and I must keep my promise to him. These were dangerous times. I would try to go back to see Agnes the following day. The villagers would get to know me soon enough. I did realise that they thought it strange I'd moved there on my own. However, they would learn how much I loved midwifery and that their mothers and babies were in safe hands with me. In that way, I would gain their respect and, if all went well, friendship would grow later. I certainly couldn't tell them I had a husband either or I'd be sent back to Greenwillows. Oh dear, I didn't like all this secrecy. But I had no choice.

Outside Agnes's cottage I saw four women huddled together, whispering. I knew that two of them were Sarah and Dorothy, the other village midwives and Rose, the innkeeper's daughter, who was about to give birth. The fourth was Jane, who I'd seen at Brockminster Hall; I heard them before they saw me.

Sarah was saying,

"That woman's taking all our work."

To which Dorothy replied,

"Yes, and she hasn't been in the village very long. We were born and brought up here. Not only that, before she came, the two of us were able to scrape a living dealing with all the villagers' deliveries. Heaven knows, I don't like the work very much, and I avoid it when I can, but Jane here loves it and helps me when she's not busy doing Lady Winchester's work."

I then heard Rose break in.

"Why isn't she married? We can see she's not pretty and likes her sweetmeats, but she seems intelligent enough and spirited, although I don't like to admit that. And why would a woman move from one village to another on her own? It just doesn't happen. I certainly don't want her delivering my baby."

Dorothy then seemed to try to reassure her.

"Don't worry, Rose, I'll be there to take care of you and your newborn."

Sarah then said something that was a little worrying.

"She must have something to hide. Have you noticed how secretive she is? We'll find out what it is somehow and let everyone know. She won't get much work then, I'll wager."

Feeling anxiety nibbling at my nerve ends, I pretended not to have heard any of this. I moved forwards, out of the doorway,

"Sorry I can't stay, Agnes." I called out loudly, "Two more babies are due, you must rest and I've got to get some sleep, too. Oh hello!"

Turning swiftly, Sarah said,

"Stealing yet another village patient, are you? Everything all right with Agnes, is it? No problems?"

"None at all, I'm glad to say." To which Dorothy added, moving a little closer menacingly,

"Wonder why Agnes would choose a stranger to deliver her baby when she's known us all her life? Haven't put a spell on her, have you? You and your cat? We all know what sort of people keep black cats."

I stretched my mouth into the shape of a smile, hoping they wouldn't see that their words were beginning to frighten me. They obviously didn't know yet, either, that Lady Winchester had asked me to take charge of the tenants' deliveries. That bit of news seemed slower than usual to uncurl into chatter.

"Bye then. Nice to see you. Take care, Rose."

Hurrying away, I heard their whispering resume until it was cut off by my rounding a corner.

Chapter 11

The following day, I decided to take a walk around Brockminster as I hadn't had a chance to get to know it very much. Settling into my cottage, paying regular visits to Lady Winchester to check her progress, as well as delivering tenants' babies and riding to Greenwillows whenever I could, had kept me very busy. Brockminster was quite a lot bigger than Greenwillows, and had more shops. Like Greenwillows, it was mainly fields and a church. But whereas wealthy Greenwillows had three Lords of the Manor who each had substantial estates, Brockminster had just the one, Lord Winchester, my parents' friend, who was a Judge.

These shops were near the Protestant church where I had, just the other day, delivered Abigail's baby, so there had been no opportunity for me to look at them then. I enjoyed looking in the windows of the butcher, fishmonger, shoe and bootmaker as well as the draper's. But my favourite was the baker's shop where I decided to buy just one small cake. Surely one little cake wouldn't make me fatter! I was very good at rationalising, and very bad at resisting temptation. Also, I'd been a bit concerned about Sarah's reaction the other day and worry seemed to walk me to the baker's!

The shop was nearly empty. However I recognised one of the customers, a cottager called George Hardacre; he was the husband of a patient of mine, Elizabeth. I liked Elizabeth but not George.

"Well, if it ishn't Mishtresh Wright. Buying yourshelf a treat, are you? Well, I can give you a treat any time you want – just shay the word. We all know how carnal women like you are."

"Thank you for the offer, Master Hardacre..."

"George, pleashe."

"Thank you for the offer, Master Hardacre, but I'll confine my attention to your good wife who needs my help, I'm sure you'll agree. How is she?"

"Oh, complaining about having two children to take care of ash well ash expecting a third. Never hash time for me, so I'm off to The Pig & Whishle."

As he left, I winked at Betty, the shop assistant, "Thought he'd just come from there!"

Finally, choosing a small, honey-covered cake, I left the shop. My heart sank as I saw George Hardacre waiting outside. This wasn't the first time he'd made a nuisance of himself, and I hadn't been in Brockminster very long.

"Come and join me at the Pig & Whishle, Mishtresh Francis. They've got rooms there, you know. Bet you haven't had any fun for a long time. Living on your own, sheeing other women'sh babies and none of your own. Musht be lonely."

This insensitive man clearly didn't realise that I wasn't interested.

"Thanks, Master Hardacre, but I'm perfectly happy on my own and love my work. Not long now to when Elizabeth will be giving you your third child. Be sure to let me know the moment it starts."

"Oh yesh. I'll be at your door quick ash a flash – maybe before the baby shtarts."

With a guffaw he stumbled off.

As I watched him go, my thoughts turned to another unfaithful man; my heart suddenly seemed to turn to stone. I had loved my husband, Arthur, so much at the start and father had treated him like the son he had never had. It was only after both my parents had passed away that I had got to know the true man behind the charm. I then discovered that he had enjoyed at least two of the pretty, young servants – who not only looked alike but had become good friends with each other, it seemed. Hannah was the one who had clearly done more than walk with him in the woods. And what about Lucy? She was as naive as I used to be. Perhaps the kindness he had shown her in getting a job at The Manor had led to other things. He could never be trusted around other women, particularly when drunk. What a fool I'd been to pursue him and mistake his ambition for love. Some said that love was blind but I didn't agree. I knew exactly how Arthur behaved and had chosen to disregard it. The blame lay with me just as much as with him. Now, the loyalty of my little black cat was all I had – and that was something I could rely on – for now, anyway.

Chapter 12

I was to see George Hardacre sooner than I'd hoped. He found me digging up borage, marjoram, caraway, thyme, mint, sage and basil for a thick soup and for scattering on the cottage floor. Rushing up to me, he said,

"It's time, it's time! Elizabeth needs you right away. She's gone into labour and insists that you deal with the birth. I'd have been happier with Sarah or Dorothy who we've always known but no, it has to be you, so get a move on and follow me. Now! She doesn't want friends or family with her either, this time. So I've asked our neighbour to stay with her until you get there."

His eyes were nearly popping out of his big, florid face so, taking my basket of herbs inside, I picked up my bag, with Precious at my heels as usual.

"Does that cat have to come as well? My neighbour's cow suddenly dropped dead yesterday. Perhaps you willed your cat to kill it. I hear that you keep toads, rats and rabbits, too, so we're wondering whether you're a hedge witch."

"Not a good idea to listen to idle chatter, Master Hardacre. It's true that I do like rabbits, although I haven't got any, but Precious would be quick to see off toads and rats."

"Hmm. Well, I'm only repeating what some of the villagers are saying. I'd watch out if I were you. After all, everybody knows how impressionable and intellectually inferior you women are."

"Yes, well, that may be the opinion of you men, but

right now I need to put my female expertise into practice and watch out for your wife, don't I?"

He then took a quick route, crossing water, and tried to grasp my hand. This man really did disgust me, taking, as he did, any opportunity to come near me.

"No, I don't need your help across the stream, thank you, in spite of the fact that it seems to be flooding these days", I said, pushing away his roaming hands. "Let's get through this watery grave of animal bones, rotting meat and human faeces as fast as we can."

"Suit yourself. Don't understand a woman who doesn't want a man around. Why haven't you got a husband?"

Fortunately for me, his wonderings were cut short as he struggled to keep his balance, slipping on the slimy stones,

"Can't you use your magical powers to get this stream to go back to its original levels?"

"If I could, I'd suggest you vanish right now, Mr Hardacre – I've got work to do."

I pushed open the door to the small cottage, put down my bag and, taking the two children by the hand, told them,

"Go and play in the garden, you two, while I help your mother. Don't wander off. I'll tell you when you can come back in."

Elizabeth's face beamed as I walked up to her.

"I'm so glad you're here. Sarah and Dorothy heard that my waters had broken and didn't like it when I said I wanted to wait for you. I want the best – not that I said that to them, of course", she added, with a grin.

When the grin turned to a groan, I helped her to the straw-filled mattress and her husband scurried away. Taking out the bottle of water, I washed my hands.

"I've heard about your magic water", Elizabeth said, glancing at it curiously.

"Don't you worry about anything except pushing at the moment. I'll take care of everything else."

"This is our third and last," she moaned as another contraction bit. "Whatever George wants when he comes home drunk, I'll just have to learn to say no."

I didn't think Elizabeth would have a difficult time, as she had had the two other live births, although I also knew that Sarah had delivered two that had died right after birth.

With the delivery almost finished, I was just about to cut the umbilical cord when Dorothy burst in, her apron covered in blood. I'd never seen her move so fast. Her demand was equally urgent.

"Rose has gone into labour and you've got to go to her right now. Jane will stay with her until you get there, then she and I will take over here. Looks as though you've almost finished anyway, so Jane can do it if I can't. Don't just stand there. Go!"

Wondering why this unfriendly woman would suddenly demand my help, I nevertheless swiftly gathered up the contents of my medical bag. When I was needed at a delivery, personal thoughts had to be put aside. Pulling down my sleeves, I heard Dorothy gasp, her intake of breath hissing around the small room. I glanced at Elizabeth, but she was beginning to fall asleep and hadn't noticed. I didn't want this woman to upset her at this fragile time.

"So you do have a mole!" Dorothy said softly, nearly stumbling as she stepped away from me. I ignored her.

"Dorothy and Jane are going to take over now, Elizabeth, you'll be fine."

She nodded sleepily.

"I'm so grateful, thank you very much."

Just as I was rushing out of the cottage, with Dorothy watching me go, I was surprised to see Hugh, who reigned in his horse to a quick halt.

"You look in a hurry. Can I help?"

My pleasure at seeing him so unexpectedly met my anxiety at needing to get to the inn. Aware of Dorothy taking in this little scene, I quickly acquiesced,

"That would be very helpful. Thank you, Hugh."

I knew this would be yet more grist to the malicious mill of the four chattering women, but I didn't have time to think about that. On the way to the inn, we had passed Jane. She was running so fast it almost looked as though she was running away from something. I felt apprehension cloak me in discomfort.

"Could we go a little faster, Hugh? Looks as though Rose is on her own."

As soon as we arrived at the inn, and, with more words of gratitude, I left Hugh to continue his journey.

Chapter 13

Clambering heavily up the inn's steps to the bedchambers, I went in. My heart plummeted. Rose was unconscious. The previously all white room was now mainly red. And as for the baby... Despair threatened to overwhelm me as I realised, for the first time in my experience, that it would probably be better if it didn't survive. Now I knew why Dorothy had demanded help. The poor little thing was half-delivered and, in her haste to get it out, she had torn off one of its arms. I had never seen such a thing before, but I knew it wasn't unusual. Many doctors didn't respect midwives as there was no formal training for us and we could only learn from experience. I'd heard, too, that Dorothy was impatient and, if a delivery wasn't going as quickly as she wanted, she became anxious. That's why she always carried a knife with her. If the baby became wedged, it either had to lose a limb when she tugged or she had to cut one off. What a way for Jane to be learning! I was beginning to realise that Dorothy was lazy and was increasingly leaving Jane to deal with her births.

Rose began to come round, but drifted off again. Stepping outside for a moment, I yelled,

"Get the Minister now!"

The inn was full, but everyone stopped talking and drinking, some spilling part of their drink, some with it half raised to their lips. All gazed at me in astonishment. Someone dashed off, but by the time the minister arrived, the badly traumatised baby had died, although Rose seemed to be rallying. I sat beside her, mopping her brow. Finally, she opened her eyes a little and gasped when she saw me.

"What're you doing here? I never wanted you near my delivery. Everything was fine until you got involved. Leave me alone! Get out! Do you hear? Go!"

I couldn't believe what I was hearing. Rose was blaming me entirely. But then, it did look as though she had been slipping in and out of consciousness, so perhaps hadn't realised when Dorothy and Jane had left. However, I did feel I needed to tell her the truth before I left.

"I'm sorry to say that everything was certainly not fine when Dorothy asked me to help, Rose."

"Dorothy wouldn't have asked you to help – she doesn't even like you. She knew very well that she was the midwife I wanted to deliver my baby. Jane was helping her, too, so we certainly didn't need anyone else."

Dismayed by this inaccuracy, sadness and overwhelming concern began to take over my whole being. I felt so very sorry about the death of this baby. Poor Rose. Although she had never been at all friendly towards me, her suffering was clear, and with that I empathised.

"I'm so sorry, Rose. Here's your mother. I'll tell her what has happened and shall leave her with you."

"I'll tell my mother myself. I want you out of here right now!"

Drained of energy, she fell back on the pillows, weeping.

I didn't want to cause her further distress, so I left, nodding to her mother on my way out, receiving a glower in return. The whole situation had upset me a great deal; all I wanted was to go home and sit by the fire with Precious. I didn't even feel like telling Marion about it. I would leave that for another day.

Chapter 14

I lay awake for a long time that night. Finally, just when I'd dozed off, I was awoken with a start by my door bursting open in the blackness. A man's voice was shouting,

"Get up – now!"

It couldn't be. Wasn't it that dreadful man, Hardacre?

"My wife's dead and it's your fault. You left Elizabeth and a newborn baby totally alone. What sort of midwife are you? A heartless one, that's what!"

I saw him stagger. He must be drunk again and using his wife as an excuse to approach me, yet again. I held the blanket between my body and his gaze. He must be wanting to join me in bed – that's what this was all about.

"What are you talking about, Master Hardacre? When I left and Dorothy took over, Elizabeth and the baby were both fine."

"What's Dorothy got to do with it? You were the midwife I took to help Elizabeth. I would've preferred either Sarah or Dorothy to have tended her, but no, she insisted that you conducted the delivery. Now she's dead and it's your fault. I can't work and look after three children. You're coming with me! You'll have to take care of all of us."

"I'm not going anywhere with you. I tell you Elizabeth and the baby were fine when I left."

"Well, my wife is definitely not fine now."

Reeling towards me, he lunged unsteadily, tearing

at my chemise. I side-stepped his grasp. It was time he was taught a lesson he wouldn't forget. Stepping forward, I hit him across the face – hard. Amazed, he stumbled backwards onto the mud floor, barely missing Precious who yowled loudly in protest. So that he knew I wasn't to be trifled with, I then stood over him and stared, long and hard. He needed to know that he had met his match and that I wouldn't tolerate his bad behaviour any longer.

"Get up! Get out of here and never come to my home again", I said quietly, but inside I was quaking. I had to make it clear that his behaviour was totally unacceptable.

As he scrambled to his feet and lurched out of the doorway, he turned,

"This time, madam, you've gone too far. This isn't the last you and your black cat have heard from me."

His words didn't frighten me, but his bullying did. He was a big man and I was small. Fortunately, on this occasion, I had caught him unawares. I would need to avoid him in future. But at the moment, all I wanted was for him to leave and never return. I stood shivering at the door and continued to stare until he was out of sight. I would try to find out what had happened to Elizabeth, but who could I ask? Marion was the only person in the village I could trust and who knew how difficult the midwives were being. It would be totally inappropriate for me to speak to Lady Winchester about it. The last thing I wanted to do was to alarm her. However, that decision was taken out of my hands.

Chapter 15

A few days later, there was a knocking on my door. It was one of Lord Winchester's grooms.

"Good morning, Mistress. I hope I find you well. Lady Winchester would like to see you this afternoon, at 4 of the clock. Unless you are otherwise engaged in midwifery, she is quite insistent on seeing you, and promptly."

"Of course. Is she unwell? Please tell her Ladyship that I shall see her at 4."

Not answering, he left as quickly as he had arrived.

Putting on my best, woollen, yellow dress that hid my repaired linen chemise underneath, I lifted the hem as I walked to Brockminster Hall across the fields. The butler, Nicholas, immediately took me to Lady Winchester and I was surprised to see that his Lordship was also there. This time there were no cakes. Although they both looked very serious, her Ladyship was as gracious as ever.

"Do come in, Margory."

"Are you well, your Ladyship?"

"I'm certainly in good health, so please don't concern yourself about that. I'll come straight to the point as I'm sure you have other work you need to be pursuing. First, I would like to say that I have always felt very fortunate in having your midwifery expertise close at hand for this, my first child."

She smiled, and I began to feel a little less anxious.

"Since my husband and I spoke to you originally, it has, of course, always been particularly important to me that you have had no deaths whatsoever among the babies and mothers you have helped through childbirth. Your excellent reputation preceded you. That is why my husband and I were delighted to put my care in your hands."

She then moved slightly so that she was able to look at me fully. Her silk gown rustled but otherwise all was quiet. I held my breath. However, one of the things I always admired about her Ladyship was her genuine, candid gaze.

"Although I've heard very good reports about your work since your arrival, I have also heard that all has not gone well each time. My husband and I would like you to clarify that. This is too serious a situation for us to take wagging tongues seriously, so we would like you, yourself, to tell us what the facts are."

So, envious chatter was raising its ugly head once again. Jane, of course, as one of the maids at Brockminster Hall, no doubt had played her part in this and was probably listening at the door as we spoke.

Lady Winchester noticed my hesitation and raised an eyebrow in anticipation. I returned her gaze equally honestly and, lifting my chin proudly, I said,

"I'm delighted to say that I have lost neither child nor mother when I have been in charge of the delivery from beginning to end."

On hearing that, her Ladyship visibly relaxed, her shoulders lowering. She smiled at me and said,

"That is all we wanted to hear, my dear. Thank

you. I felt sure that I had no reason to be concerned about your skills. One more thing. I wish to have no other than yourself and Jane present at this, my first birth. His Lordship will, of course, be close at hand, in the library."

She then rang the bell and Jane again appeared very quickly. No doubt this conversation would be received in the village before my return. Now that I was an ordinary village resident, I was learning very quickly that part of village life was such that, should I sneeze in my cottage in the morning, the other end of the village was reporting that I had a bad cold, or worse, shortly afterwards.

"Jane. Kindly show Mistress Francis out."

Turning to me, and obviously speaking for Jane's ears also,

"I'm very pleased with your visit, Margory, and shall look forward to being in your care for the remainder of my term."

"Thank you, your Ladyship. I shall see you, as usual, on Friday of this week."

"Indeed. Thank you for taking the time to come to see me this afternoon."

Chapter 16

That afternoon, I decided to call on Marion. When at Brockminster Hall, I'd bumped into Abner who said she was getting worse. The expert surgeon, whose help Lord Winchester had asked for, was visiting her occasionally but had no idea what was wrong so couldn't treat her properly. Taking some fresh herbs and vegetables from my garden I knocked on Marion's door and was dismayed to hear her croaky voice bidding me enter. I was really worried.

"My dear friend, how are you feeling?"

Marion could barely prop herself on one elbow in the bed, but attempted a brave smile, as she always did. I had never known anyone who complained as little as she did; it was easy for insincere queries about her health to be met with that same smile. But this time, I was truly shocked by her appearance. She was pale and, from what I could see, much thinner, too.

"Well, I have to say that I'm not feeling at my best. However, baby Jacob is such a joy that, when I'm with him, I forget about my illness. I think he needs to be cleaned, Margory. I'm sorry to ask you, but would you mind doing that for me. I suddenly feel as though I've no energy at all, and he's so very full of life, I'm glad to say, that today I'm in need of a little help to deal with him."

"Marion, of course, I will. You know that I'm always more than happy to help in any way I can. It saddens me deeply to see you so. I do wish that you would send a message if you're not well because I want to help as much as I can."

Walking over to little bright-eyed Jacob, he gazed at me with such a look of delighted anticipation that he didn't need words. He was clearly wanting to be picked up, which I did, pressing his soft, flawless cheek to mine. I felt such a deep swelling of love for him, I thought I would weep.

"He really loves you, Margory, that's plain to see. He sees more of you than his father who works such long hours in Lord Winchester's stables. I sometimes think Jacob doesn't know his own father at all. But that can't be helped for, when Abner is here, he plays with him a great deal and I know he loves him very much."

"Of course he does, Marion. It can't be easy for him, not being able to look after you very often and not seeing his own son very much, either. But he's a good provider and a good man. He's fortunate to work for such a fair, honest employer as Lord Winchester and to be a groom for beautiful horses in such a place as Brockminster Hall."

"Oh yes, I know, and I'm certainly grateful for that. Speaking of the Hall, although Abner refuses to listen to malicious chatter, of which there is plenty there, when he returned yesterday, he said he'd been told that George Hardacre had suddenly dropped down dead. Apparently one of his children had run to a neighbour, saying that their father was in the middle of his meal when he had fallen from his chair. As he had sought no herbs from the apothecary, nor had he displayed any signs of being unwell, it was all very mysterious. However, I thought I should tell you that, before he ate his meal, he had a visit from Sarah. When George's child was questioned about what had been said during the visit, she said she didn't know because Sarah had told them to play outside while she spoke to their father. It wasn't long after Sarah left that he fell down dead. I thought you should know, as, although you've said that he was becoming a nuisance to you, I know you wouldn't wish him dead."

Then, pulling the blanket over her shoulders, she said,

"I think that, while you're here and taking care of Jacob, I'll try to rest."

I urged her to do that. However, I was really surprised by George Hardacre's death. When he'd burst into my cottage, just a few days before, he'd certainly seemed very strong. What could have ailed him? Marion was right in saying I didn't wish him dead. On the other hand, I didn't respect him at all, nor did I like him. However, my heart went out to those three Hardacre children. First their mother, now their father. When Marion had rested, I must ask her whether they had other relatives in the village. She would know.

* * *

The morning at Marion's was spent in my favourite pursuits of playing with delightful little Jacob, as well as making sure that Marion was comfortable. She told me she felt a little better for her rest, and, before leaving, I put Jacob into bed with her. I then prepared a stew which I left bubbling in its pot on the trivet over the fire.

Leaving the cottage, I was surprised to see Sarah and Dorothy outside. On seeing me, they were quick to speak, and this time, they were much more open in their rebuke.

"Marion told you about George, has she? Well, we know what caused his death and so do you. Hope you're not making Marion more ill by your regular visits. Handsome husband, she has. And what a beautiful baby. Just the two things you haven't got. Perhaps you're wanting someone else's. Do you steal husbands as well as patients? You also seemed to be enjoying your ride behind the Judge's servant, on your way to deal with Rose's birth. You certainly do provide food for thought in the village, Mistress Francis."

"What dreadful things you say. Marion is a very good friend of mine and I'll thank you to remember that. As for George Hardacre's death. I certainly feel very sorry for the children left behind and that's all I have to say."

"Well, I found what George had to say to me very interesting just before he died", Sarah opined. "Poor man. All he wanted was someone to take care of his children when Elizabeth died. That's only natural for a bereaved father."

As these were not the truths as I knew them coming from Sarah's lips, I walked away, not wishing to involve myself further. As I left, the words "witch", "mole" and "black cat" were all I heard but I tried not to be concerned. After all, George Hardacre's death could not be linked to me in any way. Could it?

Chapter 17

Later that day, there was an urgent hammering on the door. Surprisingly, Abner, Lord Winchester's Groom, was standing there, his face wrinkled with concern.

"Mistress Francis. Master says you're to come right away. Her Ladyship has severe pains that are only moments apart. You're to ride with me."

"What? Already? The baby isn't due for another eight weeks. I'll get my bag and be right there."

Hopefully none of the troublemakers would see me riding with Abner. But all thought of them disappeared as I saw Lord Winchester's troubled face in the library doorway. Swallowing hard, I quickly entered Lady Winchester's bedchamber. I must remain calm amidst the chaos of blood-stained linen towels and her Ladyship's screams, asking whether she should prepare for death. Jane was simply standing there, saying nothing.

"Get all the towels you can, Jane, build up the fires and bring bowls for my water."

"Do you mean your magic water?"

"Get them, now, Jane!" I didn't intend to stand any more nonsense from her. I turned to her Ladyship who was screaming,

"It's coming, it's coming. Help me, help me. Thank goodness you're here, Margory. If ever your expertise was needed, it's now. Whatever made me think I could endure such pains again, for more children!"

Spasms were rippling through her Ladyship's body frequently now. Then a huge one seemed to divide the flesh between her legs, but instead of the head, I could just make out a tiny bottom. My heart sank. Not only was the baby eight weeks before its time, it was also breeched. I dug deep into my memory of breech births that my mother had performed. I could only recall one. That was when I was about 10 years old – but that was 12 years ago and had been full term. I'd never delivered a premature, breech baby. But I mustn't let my anxiety show. Not now. Not when I was needed so much. I bit my lip so hard I tasted blood.

Strands of hair clung wetly to her Ladyship's face and neck.

"Jane, hold Lady Winchester's hand and mop her brow."

"Keep pushing, your Ladyship, push hard."

At that, she became determination itself and, with a final, huge effort, the tiny little thing was ejected. Its skin was blue and covered in a thick, greasy mucus. In desperation, I blew into the miniature face. Nothing. Again, I blew, clearing away the blood. No sound.

The enormous effort of the difficult birth had left Lady Winchester extremely weak; it was fortunate that she was healthy and strong. But in the midst of this pitiful scene, she whispered,

"I want to see my baby. Why isn't it crying? Is it a boy? Is he healthy? Margory, tell me what's happening."

I had never felt such sorrow. Tears threatened to stream, but I squeezed them back. This was a sad enough scene without my adding to it. First, I had to break the news to the father – a fine man who had put all his trust in me. I had to compose myself first. I felt I had failed him. Failed his wife. The fact that it was highly unlikely any other midwife would have had a better outcome was no comfort. In their hour of need, I had failed to bring their first, new life into the world. I said a silent prayer. Merciful God, I thank you for the life of the mother who will, with your help, go on to have other children. Jane. Clear away these towels and help me to make Lady Winchester comfortable."

But Jane had disappeared. She was such a thin wisp of a girl, she seemed to come and go through walls and doors unimpeded.

I walked wearily down the wide staircase and stood in the library doorway. One look at my face and drooping body and his Lordship's face fell.

"I am so very sorry, your Lordship, but there will be no celebratory baptism on this occasion. May I suggest that you call the minister as soon as possible."

His Lordship stared at me as though in a dream.

"But you said you had never lost a child. What happened this time?"

Without waiting for my reply, he bounded up the stairs to comfort his wailing wife.

Chapter 18

My leaden feet trod a slow return path. Feeling a headache beginning to boom, I thought through the past weeks of my visits to Lady Winchester. Was there something I had failed to see? Could I have done more? Was I to blame in any way? That poor child. That poor mother. Subsumed by sadness, I was barely aware of approaching the three women who were standing near my cottage. But it wouldn't be mine much longer now.

"Galloped off on a horse with Abner, and now had to walk back. Another death? Oh dear. It's some time since you or I had a death, isn't it, Sarah. Lady Winchester is sure now to ask for the services of the midwives who were born and brought up in this village and who've served its mothers well. Jane tells us you used your magic water again. Maybe it's lost its powers, Mistress Francis, and your own skills are draining away, too, with it. Where's your cat, Mistress Francis? Maybe it had magic powers, too. But when it couldn't keep up with the horse on which you sped up to the Hall – holding tightly on to Goodwife Marion's husband, we noticed - perhaps it drowned in its own sorrows. Ding Dong Bell, Pussy's in the Well."

I couldn't bear to hear any more. Not Precious, too. I walked on in a daze, my legs seeming to have no connection to the rest of my body.

Lying on my mattress that night, I heard a soft, familiar sound and, rushing to the door, a very bedraggled cat greeted me. Thank you, thank you Lord. I looked around but no one was to be seen. He really did look as though he'd been in the well, but he was safe and sound. I rubbed him dry and he settled in front of the dying embers. But that was not to be my night for sleep. Two shapes burst through the darkness.

Chapter 19

"Get out, Mr Hardacre. Get out before I throw you out. Now!"

No, it couldn't be him. I'd been told he was dead. I must be half asleep and dreaming.

"It isn't old George, you silly bitch – or should that be silly witch! He's dead."

"Get off me..."

Deaf to my protests, the two men dragged me, kicking and screaming, across the hard, herb-smelling floor and out into the crisp, November air. My bare feet slid along the top of the frost, leaving a trail of two giant slug tracks behind me.

"Leave me alone! What's going on? Where are you taking me? Leave my cat alone!"

Too late. My shouted command sank to a whimper as one of the men booted little Precious so hard that he yowled pitifully. He flew through the air and landed with a thud. He didn't get up.

"You swine."

I threw myself at the man's neck but he was too quick and too strong for my small, heavy body.

"If you want a fight, we can go to the inn and nobody will hear your screams there. Then I'll show you who's the master. Better still, let's take her to the Brockminster Prison where everyone can join in. Nice, curvy creature like you. You deserve everything you get. We all know the sort of person who keeps black cats. Better for you that it's dead."

His growl sent shivers down my already cold,

chemise-clad spine. I said nothing more.

As I was dragged around the corner, the purpose of this black journey began to unfold before my eyes. The gallows. And that wasn't all. I had never seen the entire village altogether in one place at the same time; it wasn't a friendly sight. As the crowd saw me coming round the corner, they surged forward, baying for blood. My blood.

"Hang the witch!

I reared back and, as I did so, I began to see the few people I had come to know in the time I had spent in Brockminster. But there was no warmth there – not one friendly face. The one friend I could have counted on, Marion, was very ill and had had to take to her bed yet again. Surely the gallows weren't meant for me. What had I done to deserve such treatment? Now, even my ever-present friend, Precious, had gone. I wept silently for my loyal, feline companion.

"Let's see your magic water!"

Chapter 20

The shouts and my thoughts were interrupted by the sound of hooves. It was the elegant figure of Lord Winchester who galloped into sight, parting the Red Sea crowd. His arrival hushed them. The two men half-walked, half-dragged me to the foot of the gallows. They then stepped back, leaving the judge in charge. Here was a man whom the villagers trusted and respected - he was known to be fair. My heartbeat slowed and my shoulders relaxed a little. Although Lady Winchester's birth had been my only failure, they didn't blame me, did they?

Lord Winchester was speaking.

"We're gathered here today to examine the allegations that have been made against Mistress Margory Francis. She is said to be a witch. Not only that. A witch who has been responsible for deaths. If she is found to be innocent, she will go free. I am sorry to say that, of the three degrees of suspicion, we are considering the most serious – that of grave suspicion, which is punishable by imprisonment, torture and perhaps death. So listen to me. Owing to the gravity of the situation, no disturbance will be tolerated. He looked around the crowd.

"I call on Rose, the innkeeper's daughter. What do you have to say?"

Rose walked right up to me and glared.

"When I was giving birth, I awoke to find this woman with me. I never wanted her to be a part of my delivery and she was not there at my request. I'd said many times that I didn't want her to be my midwife. But there she was. And so was my poor, dear baby. Dead. With an arm cut off."

The crowd snarled menacingly and edged closer. I drew back. Hostility was so ripe, I could smell it.

"I said there is to be no disturbance. Thank you, Rose. Dorothy. What do you have to say?"

"Two weeks ago, Mistress Francis delivered the baby of Elizabeth and George Hardacre. When George got home, his wife was dead, their 2 children were outside, playing in the mud, and the newborn child was on its own, covered in blood and wailing. When George went to ask this woman what had happened, she tried to blame me. Me! When all I had done was to help at the end of the delivery. As George had taken Mistress Francis to deal with his wife's birth himself, he knew she had dealt with it and that his wife's death was her fault. He told Sarah that, when he went to tell Mistress Francis that she would have to take care of him and the three children, she struck him and stood over him, staring. He said he was certain she had put a hex on him, using her evil eye. As we all know, he has now died, too, having been previously fit and well. Also, she's got the witch's mark on her arm. Show us your witch's mark. We all know that's the mark of the devil. Show us!"

At the word "witch", I gasped, fear crawling through my body. It was all very clear. I was being blamed for deaths that were not my fault at all. My heart began to thud afresh. The villagers moved closer and, when one of them grabbed my sleeve, pulling it back to expose the mole, they shouted,

"There it is. That's it. The mark of a witch."

Someone else yelled,

"And what about Marion, witch Francis's good friend, as she is supposed to be. Why isn't she here speaking for her? Why? Because she's ill and close to death. Marion has a fine husband and young child – two things this evil woman lacks. Seems to me that even her best friend can't speak for her because it's Margory Francis herself who has brought an unknown illness on Marion in the hope that she can step into her shoes. As you know, Lord Winchester, even your own surgeon is mystified."

The nodding and murmurings of assent were broken by Lord Winchester.

"Mistress Francis. You have heard the evidence against you, so now we need to hear what you have to say."

Someone else shouted from the crowd,

"Never mind what she has to say. Hang her! We're not interested in what the tongue of a witch says."

But Lord Winchester was not to be shouted down.

"I repeat that we shall hear what Mistress Francis has to say. I would remind those of you here present that this is not a case of treason that is being looked at, for which legal representation is not, of course, allowed. Keep in mind, therefore, that Mistress Francis is permitted to speak for herself as well as calling on witnesses to support her, should she so wish. However, I must remind you, Mistress Francis, that the latest Witchcraft Act states that those accused of witchcraft on persons so that they die is punishable by death. What do you have to say in your defence?"

Silence fell, and Lord Winchester added,

"In that case, we shall proceed, with no further interruption."

Chapter 21

This was my last chance to set the record straight and to tell the truth.

"Thank you, Lord Winchester. I appreciate that the evidence against me must appear to be as black as my dear cat, Precious. However, I thank you for allowing me to give the facts."

"The facts of a witch with a forked tongue, you mean."

"Quiet!"

"Yes, I kept a black cat and he was a faithful friend who appeared at my door some time ago, thirsty and hungry. I would not have turned him away because some of the villagers had superstitious thoughts about him. He was just a cat.

Yes, I have a mole on my arm. It has been there, my mother told me, since the moment I was born. It did no one any harm and I have harmed no one because of it.

To those two facts, I shall add more. I am not a pretty woman and never have been. I have a hooked nose and a plain face, which some associate with witches. I am also plumper than I would like, but that, unfortunately, is because I like sweetmeats more than I should. However, more important than these facts are those surrounding my work of midwifery. Word has been whispered that I use magic water and that is why I have had no deaths of mothers or babies. And that may be partly correct.

The crowd hissed and moved closer.

"Stay back", commanded Lord Winchester. "Any

more disturbances and you will be forcibly removed from this place."

"I say it may be partly correct because the mothers and children I have delivered, as well as those delivered by my mother, were washed as soon as they appeared, with clean water that had been previously boiled. Neither my mother nor I have ever used dirty water to welcome pure new life into this wonderful world, nor to clean mothers. We have always washed our hands, too. This is what my mother taught me, and that is what I have always done. She did not attribute supernatural powers to that water and neither do I. Nor do I know whether my success in delivering live babies and keeping the mothers alive has anything to do with the water. If it does, I know not why. What I do know is that my mother had excellent midwifery skills and God has been gracious in passing them on to me. My mother loved her work and so do I. When word was passed around the village that I had had deaths of mothers and babes, you and your lady wife, Sir, being the fair people you are, asked for the truth from my own lips concerning any deaths I may have had. And that is what I gave you. The truth.

Again, there were murmurings among the crowd.

"Quiet!"

"Just as I was about to cut the umbilical cord of Elizabeth Hardacre and her baby, Dorothy appeared, asking for my help with Rose's delivery. It sounded so urgent that I immediately left her to complete that delivery – cutting the cord as well as dealing with the placenta. When I left Elizabeth and her newborn in Dorothy's hands, they were both alive. I have no way of knowing whether Dorothy stayed with her, or whether she left it to Jane to complete the birth. However, I do not wish to implicate young Jane as she is at the beginning of learning about midwifery and should not be blamed for any transgressions that occur with Dorothy's patients."

"I'm not the one who couldn't deliver her Ladyship's first child, your Lordship!"

That statement of Dorothy's was met by silence. My voice suddenly trembled, but I cleared my throat. I had tried my best in the face of that very difficult, very sad delivery.

"Finish what you were saying, Mistress Francis", Lord Winchester exhorted.

"On arriving to help with Rose's delivery, I was extremely distressed to see that the delivery started by Dorothy had not been completed and that the poor child had had an arm, either torn off or cut off. That was the situation when I got there. The baby was beyond my help with either boiled water or midwifery skills. This was another delivery that I did not conduct from beginning to end. It had been started by another midwife who, becoming anxious when things went wrong, had enlisted my aid, which I happily gave. Of course, as Rose, the mother, was in differing states of consciousness, she did not know when Dorothy had left and I had taken over, so she cannot be faulted at all for thinking that I was to blame."

At that point, I saw Agnes Fielding pushing her way to the front of the crowd, holding her child in her arms. I relaxed, knowing that there had been no difficulties at all during her delivery.

"I would like to speak."

Lord Winchester looked somewhat surprised, but motioned her to continue.

"As you can see, I have a beautiful child who was delivered by Margory Francis. And for that I am eternally grateful. I have no adverse comments to make about that. My concern is that, when I tried to begin to get to know her, she didn't allow that to happen. I think she has secrets of some kind that may have some relevance here, so I think it should be revealed. I would also like to know whether that secret has anything to do with the death of George Hardcastle, as has been described. I notice that Margory Francis has not commented on his death and I wonder why that is?"

"What are you suggesting?" asked Lord Winchester.

"Let us be honest here, Sir, we are all dancing around the possibility of witchcraft. While Mistress Francis has given her account of the events, which do sound plausible enough, she has not yet convinced me that she did not put a hex on George Hardcastle. I do wonder, too, whether that is the only secret she keeps."

I held my breath.

Chapter 22

Just when I thought Agnes would be speaking for me, she was, in fact, raising a subject for which I could not and would not give an answer. I hung my head in indecision. But glancing up, I saw the crowd begin to move. It was my good friend, Marion, shuffling very slowly to the front, leaning on her husband. My heart went out to my ill friend who should have been in bed. But here she was, and said,

"I think I can answer that."

The surprised crowd went quiet as the small, frail woman turned to face them.

"Other than Lord and Lady Winchester, I believe that I know Margory Francis better than anyone here, in this village. Knowing of her mother's fine midwifery reputation and that of Margory herself, shortly after she took the cottage on your land, Sir, I visited her and asked if she would deal with my own delivery. That was the beginning of a good friendship and, not knowing anyone in the village, Margory has tended to confide in me, too. As a result, I know that, on many occasions, George Hardcastle, rest his soul, pursued Margory, trying to take advantage of her being a woman on her own in a village that is not of her birth. In spite of Margory's making it perfectly clear that she had no interest in a man who was already wed to another, he continued to pay her unwelcome attention. Each time this happened, Margory talked to me about it because she found it very upsetting indeed. The loss of his wife must have muddled his mind – perhaps understandably

– because he then began to consider it his right that Margory would move in with him and take care of him and his three children. In making this final demand, he began to physically attack Margory, which forced her into taking the action she did. This was obviously a great shock to George, who, as we all know, has been a bully from childhood and no one had ever challenged that bullying – until Margory. It is my opinion that his growing bitterness of her spurning his advances then turned to vindictiveness and, on suddenly finding himself very ill, he decided to blame all on Mistress Francis. And he knew exactly who he should tell. He was well aware that his resentment would find favour with the other midwives' jealousy. The resulting cauldron of malicious chatter was, in fact, the only taint of witchcraft to be seen in this whole, sorry affair. I suggest to everyone here gathered that it should be the gossip mongers who should be punished, not the victim of their envy."

Marion's brave words were met with total silence and I, myself, was quite overcome by this wonderful stand of friendship that Marion had taken so staunchly. Also, I could not believe my eyes or ears. Was the Judge, Lord Winchester, actually smiling and clapping? My senses must have deceived me as, when I looked again, his face could not have been more serious.

"Well, Goodwife Marion, and there I thought I was the only Judge in Brockminster! You have shown clear judgement in stating your case here and I thank you for getting out of your sick bed in order to attempt to see that justice is carried out. Your statement has a loud ring of truth about it and gains in its veracity by Margory Francis not having spoken of George Hardcastle's unwanted actions herself."

"I now wish to consider all that has been said today before making a decision as to the fate of Mistress Francis. I do, after all, need to take into consideration the fact that Lady Winchester and I may not have engaged her services had we known that she had been present at the deaths of mothers and babies. Nor did she enlighten us, when asked. Our own experience here must play its part in my final decision."

"In the meantime, I suggest that you all go back to your labours and your cottages and put this out of your minds. While no one has ever been tried, found guilty of spiteful chatter and punished for it, perhaps I should consider making a precedent. I am particularly concerned that that type of talk may have come near to causing the death of someone."

Chapter 23

In view of the extreme distress they were causing me, I have to confess to being pleased when I saw the looks of alarm on the faces of some of the crowd. They gradually began to drift away, muttering, leaving Lord Winchester, Marion, her husband and I feeling very tired. It had been an exhausting day. At its beginning, I didn't know whether I would see the end.

Lord Winchester then said,

"I shall be in London for the next few days, and shall consider carefully everything that has been said. I suggest you come to Brockminster Hall next Wednesday, at 3 of the clock in the afternoon. In the meantime, I suggest that you go to The Manor and stay there until my return. It will be safer."

I knew what he meant, as I thought it was entirely possible that at least some of today's villagers could decide to take matters into their own hands. So I knew that it would be wise to do as he suggested. Returning to the cottage, I tidied everything and prepared the clothes I would take with me. With tears streaming down my face, I also buried dear little Precious. While doing that, I saw a number of villagers gathering again not far away, chattering and glancing towards me and began to feel some trepidation at being alone once more. However, just then, Lord Winchester's Groom, Abner, appeared, with the horse I usually used when riding to The Manor and I relaxed a little.

"Lord Winchester has told me to accompany you to The Manor, Mistress Francis."

Just as I was thanking Abner, Hugh galloped up and said,

"I'll accompany Mistress Francis to The Manor, Abner, so that you're not taken from your duties. Please tell Lord Winchester that I have told you to do that."

Making sure that I had everything I needed for the few days' stay at The Manor, Hugh then helped me on to the horse and we left, avoiding the gathering crowd, some of whom shouted obscenities at our disappearing figures.

"Are you hiding your bauble in her hole, Master Hugh? Has she put you under her spell, too?"

Pretending not to hear them, Hugh said,

"Ignore their vile words, Margory. They're not worth listening to. Lord Winchester clearly thought it likely that, in his absence, the villagers may be tempted to take justice into their own hands which is exactly what looks to be happening. Don't worry, you're in my care now and nothing and nobody is going to harm one hair of your head. I shall keep you safe until Lord Winchester's return."

I couldn't believe that someone I barely knew was protecting me in such a way. The only protection I had ever received from a man was that of my dear, late father. The feelings of gratitude coursing through my body during our ride to The Manor were beginning to grow into those of respect, trust and friendship for this good man.

As we arrived and he helped me down from my horse, I thanked him very warmly and invited him to dinner at The Manor that evening.

"I should tell you, though, that it will be a surprise to me, too, what cook will have prepared, so I hope it's to your liking."

"My dear Margory. Whatever your cook provides will, I am sure, be delicious. But above all, I shall be very pleased to share your company for the evening – and I thank you for that. In the meantime, I shall check on the work that the labourers have been doing. So until 7 of the clock then."

I blushed at his words and was reminded of the faithless man for whom I had waited, evening after evening at 7 of the clock. How very different the two men were and, indeed, I felt that I was changing, too. Perhaps my having to deal with my parents' deaths, the selfish behaviour of my husband and the loyalty of the servants had resulted in my becoming a more mature woman who was able to finally behave like an independent woman should. I certainly felt that God was helping me to deal with these traumatic times. And, of course, I still had the decision of Lord Winchester to face. However, in the meantime, I would speak to cook to see if there was a possibility of providing a fairly special meal for Hugh and me this evening. But mainly, was this excitement I felt at the prospect of spending an evening with a man I was beginning to like very much?

Chapter 24

On Tuesday of the following week, I spoke to my Housekeeper in the library.

"You will recall, I know, Goodwife Sykes, that it is tomorrow I have a meeting with Lord Winchester. As I told the household on my return, he has been considering what my fate should be and will be telling me then. While my parents and I have always known him to be a fair and just man, he knew them better than he has known me in adulthood. Also, there were a number of villagers speaking against me so, although I'm innocent of the charges, it's my word against theirs. In addition, spiteful chatter has been rife, making it very difficult to separate truth from lies. If the worst should happen, Goodwife Sykes, I have asked Hugh to let everyone know at The Manor as well as the tenants, as my punishment will be meted out immediately."

At that, I saw her eyes become moist and she touched my arm.

"Please don't say that, Mistress Margory. Everyone cares for you very much and admires the way you have managed to continue the organisation of the whole estate – with the help of Master Taylor, of course, whom we all respect and like. We all pray for you daily."

Now it was my turn to shed tears. But I had to remain strong, so, blinking them back, I said,

"I couldn't be more grateful to you and everyone here, Goodwife Sykes. However, I know that, should the worst happen, Lord Winchester and Hugh Taylor will take over the running of my parents' estate and everyone on it will be treated well. Now I must return to my duties so that, when I leave on Wednesday, everything will be in order."

That night, I slept fitfully until, at 3 after midnight, I could sleep no more. So, dressing myself, I walked around The Manor, looking with loving eyes at all the rooms I had known all my life; the walls lined with oak panelling, the carpets, so soft and gentle underfoot and the beeswax candles. It was a beautiful building that sang with the love and care it had been given, beginning with my grandparents and continued by my own parents. The removal of the silver, tapestries and paintings could not detract from the decades of dusting, polishing and cleaning that had been lavished on it. It was not the grand house visited by friends and family into which I had been born, but it was my home, and I had known no other until recently. I knew each brick, each stone. I knew each and every view from the windows, out over the beautiful fields and woods beyond our landscaped gardens. Walking slowly out into the cold night air, I crunched my way towards the woods. I wanted to look once more on the private place I had enjoyed so much as a child, the private place where I had nurtured childhood dreams of my own happy marriage surrounded by my own children. I wandered through the maze, past the fountains and topiaries. I did not regret my dreams as we all should have them. I had always reached beyond a grasp, with Heaven as my aim. I stood in the all-enveloping trees that had become my friends and thought back to when others like them had tried to warn me – of my imminent marriage and, later, of getting involved with Hannah's tended grave. I should have heeded those warnings. However, at the time, I was only interested in following my own desire. All I had wanted was a husband who I loved and who loved me, and whose many children I would bear. At the time, I had ensured that nothing and no one stood in my way. That was my mistake, and I now knew that mistakes are the doorway to discovery. But that was past and gone and, with God's help, I had learned from these errors. Now I would ask for His protection today.

I walked slowly back to The Manor, where I told cook that I had no stomach for breaking my fast; I would spend an hour's quiet time in the library. I told Goodwife Sykes that I did not wish to be disturbed and, having slid the bolt on the library door and entered my secret sanctuary, I knelt in front of the altar, perhaps for the last time. I asked for His help in being as brave and dignified as Anne Boleyn, when kneeling before the swordsman of Calais a few years before I was born, in 1536. However, my end – if, indeed, my life were to end by the noose - would not be the swift, several seconds of excruciating pain, but a more lingering death of kicking and struggling.

When I finally emerged and walked out into the great hall, Hugh was seated there, patiently waiting for me. I wasn't expecting him, but how pleased I was to see him. He told me,

"I shall ride with you to Brockminster, Margory, and, whatever the verdict, I shall be at your side."

"You're very kind to me, Hugh, but as we barely know each other, I am perfectly content to ride with God at my side."

"Then the three of us shall ride together."

And that was what we did. Hugh then left me at the door of Brockminster Hall and told me that he would be waiting for me at the end of my meeting with Lord Winchester.

Chapter 25

This time, there was no jovial welcome from his Lordship. Instead, Lord Winchester's butler, Nicholas, took my cape and hat. Knocking on the door of one of the withdrawing rooms, he announced my presence to the waiting Lord and Lady whom I approached.

"Take a seat, Mistress Francis. Lady Winchester and I thank you for being prompt. I will get straight on with telling you my decision as I wish to spare you any further anxiety. I have always found that, whatever one learns in life, be it positive or negative, just knowing what it is aids our peace of mind and I do not wish to delay that further.

When I said that I had business to attend to in London, that was only part of the reason for my visit. In fact, I had also arranged to meet an eminent surgeon who appeared to have some knowledge about premature, breech births. I told him that you had been in charge of Lady Winchester's pregnancy from the early stages and asked if you could have known of the impending abbreviated birth and of its being breech. He confirmed that you could have had no knowledge of that at all. Even more importantly, I asked if you could have done any more than you did at the time of birth. He was very strong in confirming that you could not. I know that you must be very relieved to hear that as, although I was, naturally, extremely distracted at the time, your distress was very evident.

Additionally, my wife accompanied me to this meeting and was examined by the surgeon who told her that there is no reason why she should not try to conceive again. I'm sure you can imagine that that was wonderful news for both of us to hear. Knowing you as I do, I believe you join us in that joy.

My response was immediate and heartfelt,

"I am, indeed, absolutely delighted with this news and thank you most sincerely for telling me."

Lord Winchester continued,

"I asked you to Brockminster Hall for this initial meeting as I wanted to give you that information in private, away from the crowd of villagers. However, I think it only appropriate that I should give my decision about the accusations that have been made against you separately. It is important that that decision should be given to the villagers and you at the same time. Let us leave now, as I have asked the people to gather in the market square."

Chapter 26

When I left Brockminster Hall, Hugh was waiting with the two horses. His familiar face was so reassuring to see at this frightening time. He said,

"I shall ride with you, Margory, as I don't want you to feel that you're on your own."

This was yet another example of his thoughtfulness. Again, I was struck by what a kind man he was. If I lived to see another day, I knew I could count on his friendship, and I wanted him to know how much that meant to me. In an attempt to swallow the lump in my throat, I told him,

"Thank you so much, Hugh. I can't tell you how much I appreciate your support. However, you are one of only three people in Brockminster who knows that I'm still a married woman. So in spite of the fact that I no longer see my husband nor know where he is, I think I should ride alone to the market square. I must also stand alone there to hear the Judge's verdict. If I should be found guilty – and please pray that I am not the first woman in England to be put to death for witchcraft - it will be better that you are not tainted with that shame. If I am not, there will be time enough for us to get to know one another, if that is what we both would like to do. But I do thank you from the bottom of my heart."

I saw that Hugh listened carefully to my words and his face was serious as he said,

"I must tell you, Margory, that under normal circumstances, while I would listen to your opinion and wishes, should I not agree with those desires, I would discuss it with you and would not necessarily do as you bid. However, these are not normal circumstances and I shall do exactly as you wish. I care not what others may think. I want you to know that, whatever the verdict – and I do not believe for one moment that you are guilty as charged – I shall always be there for you, and shall always be honoured to call you friend."

These words from such a good man touched me deeply and, with a smile, I began my ride so that he would not see the tears trickling down my face.

As I neared the market square, I couldn't yet see the crowd. But I could hear them. As I drew near, it was as though an orchestral conductor had waved his baton for silence. All went still. Riding to the front of the gathering, Hugh emerged, it seemed, to my distracted eyes, from nowhere and took my horse. He left equally quickly. A few moments later, Lord Winchester rode up and Hugh took his horse also. The Judge wasted no time in addressing the crowd.

"Thank you all for coming here today. I am indeed pleased to see so many of you so that as great a number as possible will know my decision from my own lips. You can then pass it on to those who are unable to be here. Indeed, this means by which news travels is at the very heart of why we are gathered here today. I do not intend to give a lecture on the subject of malicious chatter, as I think that all here are well versed in the shape of that ugly beast. Passing around news about something that has happened can be of benefit to the person it concerns, provided it is done with positive good in mind. However, gathering the detritus of incorrect facts on the way or, indeed, telling only a few of the facts that give rise to an incorrect assumption on the part of the listeners, can be dangerous. And of that we must be watchful.

I have considered carefully all the facts that were brought before me last week and that most of you here heard. I have come to the conclusion that, in each case described, presentation of only a few of the facts has led to great misunderstanding, not only for you, but for me, also. What is worse, I believe that this nasty prattling has been spread purposely and maliciously, for the attempted benefit of a few. Perhaps fear was the reason. Perhaps superstition, which raises its head often these days. I do not know the reason. What I do know is that, without the whole truth, justice is blind and I shall never, knowingly, be party to that sort of partial truth. It is for that reason that I discharge Margory Francis from all accusations brought against her."

Chapter 27

I doubled over with relief and sank to the ground, sobbing softly. I'd thought I was very close to death; now the noose had been withdrawn. In a haze, I felt arms helping me to my feet. Hugh and Abner held me close and I wept uncontrollably into their shoulders until Abner said,

"I can't tell you how happy I am to hear this very just news, Mistress Francis. Marion has had to take to her bed again, but I shall go to her now because she will be as delighted as I am."

"Thank you so much, Abner. And please do tell her that I shall come to see her as soon as I can."

It was only then that I was aware of the crowd's reaction. Some were groaning, some shouting in dismay. Whisperings snaked their way throughout the assembled group. This was a disappointing day for those who delighted in witnessing the killing of a human being. They had come, hoping to see cruel punishment meted out and must leave with that desire unrequited. They had been looking forward to watching my suffering when I twisted and squirmed, as the noose tightened around my neck. Muttering to each other, they began to slowly disperse. For my part, I could not believe my ears. I'd come to this place, knowing there was a possibility that today may be my last, and all I felt now was utter gratitude and total exhaustion. I became aware that Lord Winchester had joined Hugh and was looking down at me with a smile. Hugh's face was one of all-consuming delight. How wonderful these two men were. Lord

Winchester spoke first,

"Well, Margory, I am very pleased indeed to be the carrier of just news to you today; I'm sorry that you couldn't know my decision before. However, as you had been accused by several, I deemed it best for those people to see that justice has been done and that the verdict was as great a surprise to you, as it was to them. What I think you should do now is return to the warm arms of The Manor. You have suffered a great deal recently and it will be good for you to rest among people who love you. I would then suggest that you think about what you will do in the immediate future. At that time, I would like to meet you again, together with Lady Winchester. Take care, my dear. Hugh will continue his duties on your estate and I would like you, Hugh, to accompany Margory back there now, so that I am assured of her safety. I do not wish someone to take action into their own hands, which is quite possible. Goodbye for the moment, and I shall look forward to seeing you again, when you are ready."

With that, he pressed a purse into my hand. I was incredulous.

"Why are you giving me this, your Lordship, when my care of Lady Winchester did not have the ending any of us had wished for?"

"Because I am now satisfied that you took care of my wife, not only as well as you could, but better than most would have done. Although the result, on this occasion was tragic, I would, nevertheless, like you to care for my wife through future pregnancies."

Lord Winchester's pronouncement was more than

I could have wished for and that was a happy return ride indeed. Not only had I been spared the noose, but I continued to enjoy the trust of Lord and Lady Winchester.

My eyes were shining as we approached The Manor where the servants all came rushing out to greet me. This was a time for thanksgiving, for talk, for planning and for rest. Before taking his leave, Hugh had agreed to join me that evening.

"Cook. Let us plan a great feast. But first, I would like to enjoy a simple meal this evening for Hugh Taylor and I to share."

Sliding the bolt on the library door, I entered my secret place, went down on my knees and gave thanks. Then, on re-entering the library, I heard a knock on the door which I quietly unbolted and found Goodwife Sykes standing there, looking concerned.

"Mistress Margory. You have a visitor."

"Oh, yes, who is it, Goodwife Sykes?"

"It's me, Lucy, Lucy Topsfield, who used to be in your service. I left in circumstances that I truly regret."

Chapter 28

Of course, this was Lucy who I had asked to be companion to Hannah, my maid. How could I have forgotten her? Suddenly, it all came tumbling back. The past in Greenwillows. Just when I thought things were getting better and I was beginning to emerge from the darkness of stupidity to the enlightenment of greater wisdom, this girl had appeared from nowhere. No doubt she would dig up experiences that I would prefer to forget; I wasn't very proud of myself at that time. But I was young and naive. I could be forgiven, couldn't I? I may be forgiven, but forget, I could not. Yes, Lucy, who looked so much like Hannah. Thin, pretty, about 5 feet 1 inch tall, with long, straight, fair hair. I always had got them muddled.

I began to float back, as though in a dream, and was reminded of that other dream. It seemed so very long ago.

It was 1554, I was 14 and had just been Confirmed as, thankfully, Queen Mary had restored the old faith. I recall father, his face very serious, had said quietly at dinner a few months before,

"Elizabeth has been arrested at Ashridge Estate, and taken by barge down the Thames to The Tower. Although she's not of our faith, I wish her no ill, and can only pray that she comes to no harm."

I remembered vividly the day he was referring to as it was Palm Sunday, dark and dismal and had poured with rain, as though even the Heavens couldn't protect her. Given father's devout loyalty to our Roman Catholic faith, I thought his sentiments very generous.

After my Confirmation, my parents had given a formal celebration party to which the important local gentry, including the Cressys, Bardolphs, Neals and the Smyths had been invited. My parents had also hoped that John Brockett and his parents could come, as he was about my age and from one of the foremost families in Hertfordshire. However, my mother said the reply had said that the family, including John, would be in Italy with Francis Walsingham. I could see that she was very disappointed.

Later that day I'd gone to a hog roast that was again given by my parents, but to which our servants, tenants and demesne workers had been asked. I recalled every detail as though it was yesterday. Knowing how aware my mother was of keeping up appearances, I'd asked,

"Mother, I would really like to wear one of my more informal dresses to the hog roast. Will that be all right?"

Mother was equally generous in detail as father was in worldly matters, so she replied,

"Well, I do think as today is a special day you should be looking particularly well dressed. You are, after all, the daughter of a gentleman. However, I also want you to enjoy yourself. So let's say that if the hem of your dress gets muddy, I shall simply give it to the housekeeper to be washed."

Going to my bedroom, I suddenly felt very tired. I would rest a while before changing into my more comfortable attire. I must have been more tired than I had realised, as I instantly fell asleep and ran into a dream.

Chapter 29

The dream was about my Confirmation celebration that had just taken place and I was watching Peter who was a son of the local gentry. He was certainly handsome, but hadn't lingered long with plain, overweight me. I watched him moving easily around the room, first talking to Elizabeth, then Catherine, then Alexandra. They were all about my age and daughters of other gentry friends of my parents. What I noticed was that he looked directly into the eyes of whoever he was talking to and smiled a great deal, talking in a lively way. I noticed, too, that all these young ladies thought he was talking to them in this special way because he liked them and no one else. But that couldn't be true, I thought, because he was talking to all of them in the same way. I didn't really understand that. I'd heard a new word recently – flirting – so perhaps that was what he was doing. It was all too complicated for me.

Anyway, in my dream, Peter walked over to me while one of the servants was putting turkey and pheasant on to my plate. The strange thing was, he was dazzling me with his big, beautiful eyes that were fringed, I noticed, by thick, dark lashes, and I couldn't stop looking into them. Gazing into my own, small, brown eyes, he said,

"Let me help you with that."

As he took my plate, his hand brushed mine, sending shivers down to my toes. I'd never felt anything like that before; it was a really tingly feeling that I liked a lot.

However, when I looked at my plate of food, instead of pheasant, it had a toad sitting on it, and the toad turned to look at Peter. Not at me, but at Peter. How strange. Something else I didn't understand.

At the time, I tried to find my book of dreams and asked mother about it,

"Mother, have you seen my book of dreams?" She was in the midst of doing something else, so, waving her hand dismissively, she said,

"Speak to Goodwife Wright, our tenant, about it, darling. She's known to be good at interpreting dreams."

"Thank you, mother. That's a good idea."

I knew I would be seeing Goodwife Wright at the hog roast later that day. Truth be known, I was looking forward to the hog roast much more than the formal celebration with the local gentry. The latter were so stiff and insincere, whereas the villagers were light-hearted and merry. I knew all the people who worked on father's land, as well as their children. They were down-to-earth people whose company I enjoyed.

The only person I didn't know very well was Lucy Topsfield, who was about 11, I thought. She had been brought to The Hall very recently, mother said, by Arthur. I must ask Goodwife Wright, Arthur's mother, about her because I did like to get to know the servants.

Chapter 30

1554
Biggleswade, Bedfordshire

Lucy looked at her mother anxiously.

"Mother, you look really hot. Are you all right?"

"Oh yes, I'm fine. Making the bread seems to be making me feel more tired these days. But then, I am 30, so I'm no longer young. My old bones are beginning to be painful when I walk a long way or stand, doing the cooking. Apothecary says he's heard of a bone disease called something like arthritis but doesn't know anything about it. Says, though, that you might get it, but don't worry, it won't be for a long time yet, if at all."

Lucy gave her mother a hug, as much for her own comfort as her mother's.

"Don't say that, mother. It's probably because you've just lost another babe and are still feeling weak."

But as Lucy's cheek brushed against her mother's, it came away damp with perspiration.

"Why don't you rest a while, mother? Father will be home soon, won't he?"

"Well, the crop failure means he's having to work longer to earn less. He's doing his best."

Lucy noticed that her mother didn't mention the fact that her father now staggered into the small cottage smelling of ale. This was happening regularly and his return was usually after they had both gone to their bed. Then she noticed that her mother was staggering, too, and that had nothing to do with ale.

"Mother... Lay yourself down here."

Lucy tried to make her mother comfortable, wondering why she hadn't noticed before how thin she had become. Tears began to trickle down her cheeks as she looked at her mother's protruding bones. She cleared her throat and dabbed her eyes. Her father wasn't here and her mother couldn't look after herself, so she must take care of her. After all, she had just had her 10th birthday, so she was a young woman now. In the last two years she'd helped her mother through two miscarriages, each of which must have weakened her more than she realised. She lay down and nestled in close to her, just as she had when she was small.

Chapter 31

The hog roast was wonderful! I couldn't believe the hive of activity that met my eyes when I walked through the fields. The sounds of shouting, laughter, and even reed pipes grew ever louder as I neared this wonderful party. There were races taking place and a group of girls shouted to me,

"Mistress Margory, come and swing a hoop around your waist!" and I replied, laughing,

"In a minute. But I'm not very good!"

There were games of Hazard, Laugh and Lie Down, Nine Men's Morris and the more serious were playing Byzantine Chess. Many of the boys were playing with their bows and arrows, while others were laughing and joking, swimming in the river. Even the little ones were joining in, with some of them on wooden horses and wielding whips! Everyone was enjoying themselves and I couldn't wait to join in. And yes, my dress became muddy and torn, but just a little bit, so I hoped mother wouldn't be too cross. I also tried hard not to pile my plate quite so high – but that wasn't easy, either. I knew that I would never look as beautiful as our neighbours, Elizabeth and Catherine so what did it matter.

I did like to know which of our tenants had had babies – I adored little ones - and I tried to get to know all the children. Looking around at the happy throng, I was a little startled – and distracted! - to notice Goodwife Wright's son, Arthur, who was about 2 years younger than me. I hadn't realised what a handsome boy he was becoming, with his pale hair, big blue eyes and beautiful smile. He was also much taller than me, and that was something I particularly liked in a boy. It was surprising that I hadn't really noticed him before. He was talking to two pretty girls who looked so alike perhaps they were twins.

Suddenly I noticed that Arthur's mother, Goodwife Wright was standing on her own. This was my opportunity to ask her advice about my dream.

"Oh hello, Mistress Francis, I'm so pleased to see you enjoying yourself. I was just sitting here thinking what a lovely day you must have had. First, with gentry friends of your own kind and now, you do seem to be having a good time with us, too. You're growing into a fine young woman, if you don't mind my saying, Mistress."

"You're very kind, Goodwife Wright, but, in fact, I'm enjoying myself far more here, with the tenants and your children, than I did at the formal party my parents generously gave me earlier today."

"Well, be that as it may, I'm sure you're looking forward to the day when you're mistress of your own manor house. But you look as though you're wanting to ask me something. How can I help you?"

"Well, I had a very strange dream last night."

When I'd finished telling her all about it, I noticed that she looked a little concerned, but quickly brushed away the look, so I wouldn't be upset, I supposed. That made me even more curious.

"Dreams are very funny things, Mistress Francis, and different people put different interpretations on them, so you're not to be concerned about what I have to say, because somebody else might say something different to you. Now I really was intrigued, and replied,

"That's all right, do tell me please."

I knew that Goodwife Wright was a caring person and wouldn't want to worry me, but I did want to know what she thought. I also knew that she was one of the best interpreters of dreams on father's land.

"Some people are what's known as charming, Mistress Francis, and that's fine, just so long as other people realise that it doesn't necessarily mean that they're only being charming to them, if you see what I mean. Then there are charming gentlemen who charm ladies other than the lady they're with, even if they're betrothed or married to them. This can mean that, sometimes, their lady's feelings are hurt because the lady he is charming thinks that he wants to be with them and not their betrothed or wife. Also, it can sometimes go further than that, but I don't think you need to hear about that."

"Oh please do tell me, Goodwife Wright, because I would really like to know what my dream meant and I know that you're very good at interpreting."

"Thank you. Well, a toad in a dream means infidelity and infidelity means that someone is unfaithful to you. That is, they are deceitful and disloyal. Begging your pardon if I'm speaking out of turn, Mistress Francis, but everyone knows that your parents love each other very much and one would never be unfaithful or disloyal to the other because neither would want to hurt the other."

"Yes, and you and your husband love each other

very much, too, Goodwife Wright, don't you, so your husband would never be unfaithful to you either?"

"Mistress Francis, I'm delighted that my eldest son, Arthur, has taken up service at The Manor. Although I say it myself as shouldn't, he's a clever boy who can do much more than working in the fields, scaring birds, picking stones and casting seed in the furrows. Between you and me, it'll also mean that he won't start going to the inn with his father, which pleases me. He gets on with folk, does our Arthur. In fact, just the other day, when he was walking home from the fields, he came across a young girl sitting in one of the hedgerows crying her eyes out. Only a scrap of a thing, she was, all skin and bones."

I'd noticed, of course, that Goodwife Wright hadn't replied when I mentioned that she and her husband loved each other and wouldn't be unfaithful. I hoped that was only because she'd started to tell me about Lucy. She was such a nice person and I wouldn't like to think of her being hurt if a toad had crept into their lives. Ugh! I liked frogs but toads were not nice creatures. But maybe I didn't like them because they were ugly – and they couldn't help that, any more than I could help being plain.

I was returned to what she was saying as she was continuing to tell me about Arthur and the new servant, Lucy.

"Arthur said that when he sat down next to her she was a bit frightened, but it turned out her mother was dead and her father had run off. She told him she was an only child and was walking to London to find work. She said she'd walked from Biggleswade, so it's no wonder she was weary and her shoes had holes. Gone are the days when it was thought – and taught – that our Christian duty was to feed the hungry, give drink to the thirsty, welcome a stranger, clothe the naked and visit the sick. The poor girl had been left to cope for herself.

Arthur told her that London was no place for a young girl, so he brought her back here. I think he feels quite protective of her, being all on her own. That's a quality I haven't observed before in my Arthur, and it was very pleasing to see. Anyway, I took one look at the poor little ragamuffin, with her dirty hair and clothes, told Arthur to get more vegetables from the garden and gave her a good wash. She looked quite different when she was clean! She's a pretty little thing, with her big eyes and long hair; suitably humble, too, which is always a trait I like to see in a young girl. I noticed that Arthur was looking at her appreciatively, too. Our Arthur always was easily tempted by a pretty face, and at The Manor there's more than one of those among the servants. But that's of no interest to you, of course. Anyway, you should have seen how fast she ate all the potatoes and vegetables I put in front of her. Like she hadn't eaten for weeks! Maybe poor soul hadn't, either. Then she slept and slept and slept like she'd never wake up.

Finally, she got up and looked so happy I gave her a big cuddle. She said she wanted to work for me, doing anything at all. I told her I had no money to pay her, to which she said that didn't matter. But she seems a cheerful girl, and hard working, I'd wager. However, in spite of the fact that I felt she was trustworthy, I nevertheless asked her if she'd turned to doing anything wrong, like stealing, on her journey. I told her that if she had, it would show itself some time, in some way, such as a sudden limp. She assured me that she hadn't, but then she hesitated a moment. She said that she'd nearly forgotten that one day, on her long walk, she'd been so hungry she'd taken two apples from a tree she'd come across. When I asked if that was all she'd taken, she looked at me in such an open, honest way, that I knew it was. She told me she'd tried to get a begging licence in Biggleswade, but couldn't, and didn't know anybody who could get one for her, either.

The next day, I suggested she went to The Manor with Arthur to ask if she could help there. Your housekeeper said they needed another scullery maid and as she was used to helping her late mother wash the dishes and laundry, that has worked out fine. In fact, Goodwife Sykes says she's so good at her job and gets it done so fast that she came to her the other day asking what else she could do – and that doesn't happen very often!

It just so happened that your mother was on her way out to check on another of the tenants who's expecting her fifth any day, she had called for you but wasn't sure where you were, so Lucy went with her. 'Course, she couldn't help with the birth itself, and your mother told her not to watch anyway, if she was at all frightened. So she kept boiling kettles and making sure there were lots of towels there. Same as you did when you first started helping your mother. Now you're quite the little expert yourself. But Lucy's new to it and told her Ladyship that she had really enjoyed it.

She comes to visit me sometimes, when she isn't working. She's quite shy, but she's gradually telling me how her mother had become ill. That was when Lucy had to start washing clothes, dishes and anything else really. She said there was no money so she was growing as many vegetables as she could. Then, she said that, one day, she came in from their little garden and her mother was wriggling about on the floor, sweating and muttering strange things. Lucy, poor thing, says she was really frightened, ran to their closest neighbour who took one look and said she wasn't going near her mother. So Lucy sat there, for several days. Says she doesn't know how long it was, just that the sun kept going down and coming up again. She tried to keep her mother's temperature down by bathing her in cold water, but it didn't seem to help. First her mother was sweating, then cold and was becoming delirious (she didn't know that word, but told me her mother started babbling strangely) and developed a red, bumpy rash on her face and forearms. When that happened, no one came to see her at all.

One morning, she said she awoke, lying next to her mother who wasn't moving and was blue and cold. Lucy says she had never seen anyone dead, but her mother's eyes were open and she knew she'd gone. When she went to the apothecary, he said it sounded like something beginning with "p" or "n", so it must have been pneumonia. Of course, word had spread that there'd been two cases of bubonic plague in London, so who knows what it was. But when Lucy's mother had started to get the rash, her father had left, leaving Lucy on her own. The apothecary said he would arrange for her mother to be taken away; Lucy was so upset she didn't find out where she was going to be taken. She went for a long walk, prayed, and when she got back, her mother wasn't there.

As she hasn't got any brothers or sisters, she thought she'd better find some sort of work, so started walking. When night fell, she climbed into ditches and slept under hedges, which explains why she was so dirty and scratched when Arthur saw her and brought her here. Seems to me to be a dear girl without anyone in the world to look out for her and no money either. But I suspect she'll do her best to please Goodwife Sykes. Also, if she can help your mother sometimes with the birthing, she will. She told me she really enjoys that and, although she doesn't think she's clever enough to ever be a licensed midwife, she seems to be happy just helping your mother in any way she can. Your mother is such a good woman that I know she'll teach Lucy whatever she thinks is appropriate. I'm also really pleased to see that Hannah and Lucy are becoming good friends. And don't they look alike?"

I was interested to hear about Lucy's previous life because I'd wondered where she came from and where her family was. As an only child myself, I couldn't imagine what it must be like to lose both your mother and father, as Lucy had done. But at least, if it happened to me, being the only daughter of a wealthy landowner, I would never be poor financially – or so I thought. I just didn't think that could ever happen to me because the land had been inherited from my grandparents and was totally safe. What must it be like to have no parents and no money? What a dreadful thought!

I was startled out of my reverie by Goodwife Wright's cheery words,

"Here's Arthur hoping for a dance with you. Off you go, Mistress, and don't worry your head about dreams and toads. You're awake now, so go and enjoy yourself."

I did enjoy that dance. Who wouldn't like being near a tall, handsome young man? I certainly did. But, as it began to get dark, I said goodbye to everyone.

Chapter 32

Walking back to The Manor, I thought about my dream, toads and a few other things. I'd enjoyed seeing all the tenants' children again, but perhaps particularly Arthur. I was also pleased to hear a little about our new servant, Lucy.

Arthur had asked me to stay longer, but I said that I must be getting back. I knew that mother was expecting me before sunset, so I'd promised I would see him another day. But I felt a pang of what? Jealousy? When I noticed him turn away and ask Lucy to dance. Or was it Hannah? I just couldn't tell them apart. Dreams and toads, dreams and toads.

Arriving home, I rushed into one of the withdrawing rooms,

"Mother, mother, I've learned a new word."

"Oh good, what's that, darling?" she asked, smiling at me.

"In-fi-de-lity."

As I was pronouncing the word, I noticed that my mother's face slowly lost its smile as she turned,

"Darling. Who told you that word and why?"

"Well, I spoke to Goodwife Wright about the strange dream I had had and what she thought it meant because I'd heard that she's really good at giving reasons for dreams. Mine was about a toad which Goodwife Wright said was about infidelity."

"What did Goodwife Wright tell you about the word?"

"Well, she said that it's when two people who are

together don't love each other as much as you and father do and that one of them – and she said that it's often the man, but not always – hurts the person they live with by loving someone else."

"Yes, that's right, Margory. Some people are hurt in that way and it isn't a pain that goes away, so I'm very pleased that your father and I love each other and wouldn't think of hurting each other, in that way or any other. Sometimes people behave differently when they go to the inn and drink a lot of ale, too, and that's when there can also be difficulties, only one of which is gambling."

I noticed that mother didn't say that Master and Goodwife Wright didn't hurt each other in that way, so, once again, I hoped they were happy together. I did know, though, that Master Wright went to the inn quite a lot, so perhaps that's what mother meant. Perhaps he drank and gambled – but I knew nothing of these things. It was a bit of a mystery, really. Who would've thought that my dream about toads would uncover all these things about Master and Goodwife Wright as well as mother and father?

Chapter 33

I was very tired indeed at the end of my very special day and, after giving mother and father a big hug and kiss and thanking them for giving me such a wonderful time – not one, but two parties - I said that I'd like to go to bed after bathing. I think that they were tired, too, as I heard them talking softly as they climbed the stairs. I thought I heard father saying that maybe I should have been a boy, but I couldn't be sure. I certainly enjoyed running around, playing games, at which times my flowing, silk dresses did get in the way.

I drifted off to sleep, thinking how lucky I was to have such kind, loving parents. I wondered if I could eat a little less from tomorrow? I would try, for mother's sake. Maybe if I was thinner, the handsome sons of our gentry friends would be more interested in talking to me. While I knew that curvaceousness was fashionable, I could probably be described as fat. On the other hand, I couldn't do anything about my big nose, so maybe I would just eat what I enjoyed eating. I started to drift asleep, thinking about my favourite foods and wondering what I would dream about tonight.

Chapter 34

1556

"Was that someone calling, mother?"

"No, my dear. Were you expecting anyone?"

"No, not really. But I did wonder whether any of the young men who came to my Confirmation might ask me to walk out with them. I know that the Bardolphs are having a ball, and I wondered whether an invitation had arrived for me?"

"I'm sorry, dear, not yet. I'll let you know the moment we do receive one."

I tried not to feel too disappointed that none of the local gentry's sons seemed to be interested in me. Gradually I began to wonder if I would ever meet a man to fall in love with, who loved me and to have a family of my own. I did so want those three things very much.

I'd known that Arthur Wright was now working at The Manor, of course, and was always aware of him when he was around; he was so tall and handsome. I noticed that all the female servants were aware of him, too. I didn't like that very much. When I saw him talking to a pretty maid, I got a funny feeling inside.

My personal maid, Hannah, had told me that he'd walked up to The Manor and, when our butler asked him the nature of his business, he said he'd like to speak to the Master about a private matter. He was told that the Master was busy but that he could speak to his manservant, Stephen. I was to learn later that Arthur had said that, rather than take an apprenticeship in husbandry, he wanted to join the household in whatever capacity he could and that, eventually, he would like to work directly for my father. For a boy so young – for I think he was then only 14 - such courage and confidence had, apparently, impressed the now ageing Stephen who, later that day, had told my father all about the incident.

On Lady Day, therefore, Arthur had started his contract of employment and had proven true to his word, working hard and learning all about the work of each and every one of the servants. I would see him sometimes, doing the bidding of the housekeeper, cook and Giles, the butler. Increasingly, I saw him helping Stephen who, I thought, was beginning to rely on him more and more. For my part, I found his presence very pleasant and felt my heart leap a little one evening, after dinner. Father had looked up from his reading and, mainly addressing mother, said,

"That boy, Arthur, is a very hard worker. Strong and courageous, too. He's becoming a real asset. At the moment, he returns to his parents to eat and sleep, but I'm considering asking him to join our servants for meals so that he is better fed. Would you speak to cook about putting out another trencher, and I'll speak to Arthur about it tomorrow."

Mother's look of surprise was lost on father, but not on me.

"Don't forget, darling, that he's from quite a different social background and may be embarrassed to join a table, the manners of which are not what he has known."

"Embarrassed! Not that boy. I'll wager that he'll

quickly learn all that's necessary about table manners from the other servants. If we had been fortunate enough to have our own son, I would have wished him to have the sort of confidence, intelligence and charm of Arthur. No, in spite of his lowly beginnings, he will go far and I would like to encourage him in that."

As father rarely referred to her not having borne a son, her response was understandably quick.

"Of course, my dear. I really don't know him very well and you do. I think you know him a little, too, Margory, don't you. What do you think of him?"

Suddenly drawn into the conversation to which I had been listening intently, I hesitated, blushing,

"I think he's a very agreeable young man."

Not noticing my reddening face, father said,

"That's settled then. I shall speak to him tomorrow. Normally, I would ask Giles to speak to him, but I've taken a liking to Arthur, so I shall do it myself."

Unfortunately, my blushes had not gone unnoticed by mother, so, when father had left us alone, she came and sat by my side.

"As both you and your father have said that Arthur is growing into a fine young man, I'm sure that is the case. You, in particular, Margory, have got to know him a little, as his brother, George, was the first birth you witnessed and you have seen him and his family regularly since that day. However, I would like you to remember that his birth and upbringing are very different from your own. You are the daughter of a Gentleman, a Gentleman who has inherited several hundred acres of land from his father and his father before him. I, myself, am also the daughter of a Gentleman in Greenwillows. Your father has considerable influence in local politics and our friends are from similar backgrounds. That is why we socialise with gentry such as the Brocketts and the Smyths. You have been taught how to read and write as well as to appreciate art and music, so I know that, some day, you will make a member of the gentry an excellent wife who knows how to manage a large household.

It may be that you think it is inappropriate for me to speak to you this way. However, Arthur is a very good-looking young man and I have noticed the way in which you look at him sometimes. When he joins us for meals in the dining room, he will do so by joining the servants at the other end of the table, as you know. He will join the servants because he is the son of a tenant and I would like you to keep that in mind. That is all I have to say at the moment, dearest, but I would like you to think about my words. I know you are an intelligent young woman and I hope that you will exercise common sense, also, in this matter."

Mother's lengthy speech – because that is the way I regarded it – was very unlike her, so I knew that she was serious about what she was saying. I would need to think about it because I certainly was becoming increasingly aware of Arthur whose smile brightened my day. However, I was unsure how many days of others he also brightened; I'd noticed many young, pretty girls in our household looking at him also, in particular Hannah and Lucy.

At the moment, though, it was very easy to heed

mother's words, as, although our paths had crossed occasionally, Arthur and I did not know each other very much at all, really.

Chapter 35

So the following day, Arthur joined the other servants at the table, for breakfast, mid-day and evening meals; suddenly I was seeing him much more closely and frequently. Of course, I didn't take breakfast as early as the servants, so I only saw him at the other two meals. However, I grew used to seeing his tall body – he must have been about 6 feet 2 inches – curl itself into a chair, saying,

"Is anyone sitting here?" to which he always received shy smiles accompanied by "No, we thought you might like the seat."

And that wasn't all I noticed. He was lithe of body with fair hair that he left to grow to just above shoulder-length. His blue eyes seemed to look everywhere and see everything – and always had, since he was young. But mainly, I noticed his smile that began very slowly and, at its widest, awoke two deep dimples. How I loved to see those dimples coming awake for me. It seemed that, now, whenever I glanced towards the servants' end of our very long dining table, he would stop his conversation, look me directly in the eye and I would see that smile and those dimples. I also noticed that the discussion he curtailed was with either my maid, Hannah, or our new servant, Lucy, who seemed to always occupy the seats on either side of him, listening intently to his every word.
Suddenly I was shaken out of my day-dreaming by mother,

"Margory, your father is waiting for an answer!"

The note of admonishment was clear in her voice

as I realised that father must have spoken to me. Feeling as though I was in another place, with only Arthur and me in it, I dragged my thoughts away from his face.

"Sorry, mother. I didn't hear what father said."

"In spite of his saying it twice!"

Now mother was annoyed and I was rarely the cause of that so I looked at father.

"I'm sorry, father. Did you say something to me?"

"Indeed I did, my dear. Your mother and I think that it will be a good idea if you take a holiday for a short while. As you know, your aunts and cousins are visiting us next week from Gloucestershire and your aunt Juliana has invited you to stay with them for three months."

I groaned inwardly. Three months! And going so far away from... My thoughts moved quickly.

"Oh, dear father. How could I be separated from you and dear mother for so long? It would break my heart. I have never, ever been parted from you at all. Is there a reason why I am to go for so long? Then on reflection. I help mother often when she is delivering the tenants' babies – whose numbers are increasing rapidly - as well as when any of them are ill. Mother will miss my help and it won't be so easy for her to tend the tenants. Also, I shall miss seeing these newborns so much. Although I shall certainly enjoy seeing my cousins and aunts, do I really have to go for such a long time? I shall miss both of you so very much." Mother was equally quick to reply, and in her most determined of voices.

"And I shall certainly miss you, darling, because you are very helpful. Also, your midwifery skills are becoming very good indeed. However, I have spoken to Lucy who has had a little experience of deliveries and would really like to help me, in your absence. It will do you good, my dear, to see another great house, get to know your cousins better and go to balls with them. You spend a great deal of time here alone, as you have no siblings. That is a regret of mine. However, this invitation from my sister allows me to rectify that somewhat. You'll have an exceedingly good time and it's very kind of your Aunt Juliana to invite you."

So that was it. It had all been discussed and decided beforehand and I had no choice but to go. I certainly liked my aunt and cousins, but Gloucestershire was such a long way from The Manor and my parents. In my heart of hearts, though, although certainly I knew that I would miss mother and father, I couldn't bear the thought of leaving behind that fair head, those wondrous eyes and, joy of joys, those smiles. But go I must, it seemed.

Chapter 36

"I thought she'd never go! Come on, Hannah. I want to show you a part of the woods that will be our place, and our place only. The trees are really thick and the moss is very soft. Just right for us to lie down on together."

"Oooh, I don't know, Master Arthur. Lucy said she'd cover for me if anyone asks where I am, but what if Mistress Margory finds out?"

"So what if she does? All I have to do is smile at her and she melts like the snowmen I used to make as a child. Truth is, her face is so plain I can barely bear to look on't. It's no wonder none of the local gentry come a-calling. But enough of her. It's your pretty face I want to look upon. Here we are. This is the place. Now just lie down and pretend you're in Heaven."

"Oh, Master Arthur, you say such lovely things."

"Well, let's stop talking and start looking – at each other. You're beautiful, Hannah. Has anyone ever told you?"

Chapter 37

Dear Diary,

It's early evening and we've just arrived in Gloucester, having left immediately after breaking our fast this morning. I've asked if I may retire early as I'm very tired. We were mainly an all lady party, except for two cousins, Robert and Cecil, who are 20 and 23 and who would, I'm sure, have fought valiantly to save our possessions, should we have encountered thieves. I've asked Aunt Juliana if, tomorrow, I may go to Gloucester's Cathedral to give thanks for our safe deliverance and she has said that we shall all go. I shall also pray to be allowed to return to The Manor in less than three months as I just cannot bear the thought of not seeing Arthur. There, I've said it to you, my diary. And, of course, mother knows that I enjoy looking at him, but only you know how deep my feelings are becoming now. I can confide in you that I know not whether Arthur has feelings for me. All I know is that he does look at me sometimes and, when he does so, he smiles, and that is enough for now. One day soon, I intend to be the only girl on whom he bestows that special smile, and I look forward to that day with delight.

* * *

Oh, my time with Aunt Juliana and cousins Ellen, Edith and Emma was very pleasant and, yes, mother was correct when she said that the change of home and scenery would do me good. It was very enjoyable indeed to have the company of my three cousins on a daily basis and, on the first day of my visit, Ellen asked,

"Do say what you would like to do, Margory. We could walk and talk about the latest fashions. Mother has arranged several balls while you're here, so I'd love to show you what I'll be wearing. Or perhaps you'd prefer to read or continue with your tapestry, which I think one of your maids carried with her."

Then, more conspiratorially,

"There is one young man who I find particularly handsome and who I know will be going to at least one of the balls. Do tell me, Margory, if you find one of the young men to your liking."

"Er. I shall, Ellen, the moment that happens."

I did so try to enter into this sort of conversation wholeheartedly with my cousins. But, as Arthur was rarely out of my thoughts, and in spite of the fact that we were not walking out together, I felt it would be disloyal of me to look forward to meeting these young men. After all, I was beginning to give my heart to him, even though he didn't know it yet.

As time went by, I also missed other things about my daily life in Hertfordshire. Like helping our tenants with mother, listening to my parents' discussions about politics, as well as my father's visits to London to discuss his work about the poor with William Garrard. I missed my own, private place in the woods where I would lay down and feel that the woodland around me was my real home and the trees and animals, my friends. But mainly I missed seeing that smile.

Chapter 38

Those three months were very long indeed; how fickle was time. I marvelled at how half-an-hour in the company of Arthur seemed to pass in seconds, whereas one single month away from him felt like a whole year. I had known from the start, of course, that mother was hoping I would forget him. I think she even hoped that I would meet a Gentleman – a member of my own social class – and fall in love with him. I did wonder, though, how she could consider the thought of my living so far away from her and father. After all, even when the weather was good, it was an entire day's ride. But I came to the conclusion that she would prefer to see me in the company of someone of my own social standing, some distance away from home, than in Hertfordshire with a man who was beneath me (as she thought). But really, unless Arthur was found to be a bad person, why shouldn't we start to spend time together? I really didn't understand. Didn't love conquer all?

Chapter 39

Finally, and to my great relief, the visit to my relations came to an end, but I didn't want to sound ungrateful. It had been pleasant to spend time with my cousins. But I was used to being on my own and didn't find it easy to listen to constant conversation from morning 'til night.

"Thank you so much for everything, Aunt. I've had a wonderful time."

We kissed and I was on my way home. Immediately, my spirits lifted.

One of my male cousins and one of the grooms rode back with me to Hertfordshire and stayed with us for a night before returning to Gloucester. So the first time I was to see Arthur, without the distraction of others, was at dinner, two days after my return. I worried that he might have forgotten me. I worried that he may have met and started seeing one of the servants or tenant's daughters. But surely the daughter of gentry was to be preferred to these other, more lowly creatures. But I did worry, nevertheless. After all, three months was a very long time and anything could have happened.

Chapter 40

What should I wear to dinner that evening? Mother would notice if I wore something more special than usual, particularly if it was rather revealing. I may be plain, but my figure, I knew, was quite voluptuous. I'd noticed that, while men didn't seem to be interested in looking at my face, their eyes did linger on my breasts, so I was beginning to learn to buy dresses that accentuated this one redeeming feature. While staying with my cousins, my aunt Juliana had suggested very thoughtfully, when we were alone in the drawing room one day,

"Margory, my dear, while you are away from home, I think this will be a good opportunity for you to buy some new dresses. But before we do that, I shall ask cook to serve lighter, smaller meals for you. What do you think?"

What I thought was that my aunt was being very diplomatic. However, as I didn't feel like eating very much anyway, I was happy to agree. So in the three months' absence, I had gained the more fashionable figure of curvaceous, rather than being overweight, which, I noticed, suited my small frame well. To enhance my new shape, I'd followed my aunt's suggestion of buying several new dresses, two to be worn during the day and two for evening occasions. Two were fairly plain, while two were embroidered with gold thread and were very beautiful. The most expensive dyes had been used and I'd chosen bright red, two in purple and one in indigo.

I asked my maid, Hannah, to get out the indigo one, which I thought suited my light brown hair and brown eyes.

As she was lacing the stiff bodice at the back, there was a knock and mother came into my bedchamber. I watched her face closely, hoping that she was unaware of what was on my mind.

"Tomorrow, I would like to see the dresses you bought in Gloucester, my dear. The letter my sister sent with you said that they are the latest fashion and compare favourably with London fashions. I see you are looking thinner, too, which suits you. In fact, darling, you look very well indeed and better than you have looked for quite some time. The Gloucester air must have done you good. Indeed, in your absence, the weather here in Hertfordshire became sunny and bright, but has reverted to being stormy since your return, which is strange. However, I shall write to Juliana to both thank her and to say that I would like to take up her invitation of hospitality to you on another occasion, not too far distant."

"Thank you, mother. I, of course, left a letter of thanks with my aunt as she was a very generous and considerate hostess. However, I did miss you and father very much. Not only that, I missed our tenants as I know so many of them extremely well. In particular, I was very sorry to miss the births with which I would normally have helped you. I do hope you haven't replaced my help permanently."

"Of course not, darling. Not only do I enjoy teaching you midwifery skills, but you also show a natural aptitude for delivering babies. Although we haven't spoken of it before, I hope this is something you will continue when you are mistress of your own estate and are married to a Gentleman. However, Lucy was very helpful and took on any task I asked."

My heart sank. Mother was still hoping that I would meet a Gentleman when, in fact, none of the local gentry had shown any interest in me whatsoever, nor I, in them. A slow smile and deep dimples kept springing to mind and I blushed a little at the thought. Noticing my rising colour, mother assumed the cause was her reference to my marrying a Gentleman – surprising, as she was usually so astute.

"You're looking very pretty, my dear, and, while you may not think that you have been the focus of attention of any one Gentleman in particular, that may be about to change. My sister has told me that one, extremely well connected Gentleman was seen to cast more than one look in your direction."

I shuddered at the thought. I knew the Gentleman to whom she was alluding. I am small in height but he was smaller; three months ago, I was round, but he was even more so. Also, I had never seen such unattractive table manners and had wished that my aunt would stop placing me opposite him at the dining table. Whenever I glanced up, he had food hanging from his mouth and, on seeing my glance, he would open his mouth to smile, revealing a very full mouth indeed. On closing it again, some of that food was constantly dribbling from its corners. I had wondered at the time how anyone could consider approaching that mouth, which only seemed to be happy when it was eating and full. Any other function would have been out of the question, certainly for me.

"Yes, mother, the Gentleman in question was, indeed, very well positioned in society and has been for all the 50 years of his life." Mother was quick to respond,

"Age brings wisdom and experience, my dear. Also, affection usually develops in the coming together of those in the same social class. But let us not spoil your first dinner with father and me. As we would like to hear all about your three months in Gloucester with your aunt and cousins, I have asked all the servants to take their evening meal in the kitchen."

I had just applied what my cousins had told me was the latest fashionable red lip colour and was standing back to admire the overall effect. I then did something that was even a surprise to me. At mother's words, my newly slender body spun around, my silk skirt rustling like the autumn leaves, my breasts heaving. The blood red slash that was my opened mouth seemed to wish to swallow my mother whole and she gasped, half falling back against the bedroom wall. I could see she was thinking that this was not the daughter she had sent away three months before; her horror-stricken face froze. At the same time, she clutched her heart and the scene, as though from a play, reverted to the way it had always been – that of conciliatory daughter.

"Mother. Are you all right?"

I hurried to help her to the nearest chair.

"Hannah, get some cold water and smelling salts – hurry."

Mother's face had paled, her eyelids were

fluttering but, above all, her face had taken on such an extreme look of sadness that I suddenly felt very guilty. Never in my life had I caused either of my parents any sort of alarm or anxiety. What had made me turn on mother in that way? My action seemed beyond my control, as though a different person had momentarily taken possession of my body.

Sipping her water, mother gradually began to relax, stopped clutching her heart and her eyes opened wide.

"Mother, why are you looking at me like that? I didn't intend to cause you anxiety, truly I didn't. I don't know what happened, but suddenly my actions seemed to be those of someone else entirely."

"I'm very glad to see that you have recovered your composure, Margory. I certainly do not wish to see a display of temper like that ever again. I have only seen such a rapid change of character once before in my lifetime and that person turned out to be a wi..." Mother paused.

"But let us put this unpleasant incident behind us and forget that it ever happened. Father will be waiting and he is not the most patient of men."

As we descended the stairs to the dining room, mother a little stiffly and I, suddenly exhausted, I joined her in wondering what had caused my unexpected emotional outburst. I loved mother and father and would never do anything to cause them anxiety or harm. But the person who had reacted did not seem to be me. My extreme annoyance on hearing that mother had, yet again, taken steps to keep Arthur and I apart had taken over my mind, body and soul so that I had become someone unrecognisable, even to myself. The disappointment felt by me, Margory, had turned into the extreme rage of someone I did not recognise at all. It was as though I had stepped outside myself and become someone I did not know. But it sounded as though mother had seen something similar before. Who could that have been and what had they turned out to be?

Chapter 41

The following day, everything had returned to normal. When I went down to join my parents to break our fast, the servants had already taken theirs and had left. It was a beautiful morning so I decided to take a walk around the land, calling in to see the tenants, catching up on what they had been doing and how they were. My first call was to Arthur's mother who was spinning. Although father paid his workers well, Arthur's mother was just one of many wives who also had to contribute to the household's finances, particularly as the numbers of children increased – and this could be up to five or six. As always, she was very cheerful and, getting up, she said,

"Welcome back, Mistress Margory. You look very well indeed. The Gloucester air must have been good for you, but you have been missed here. Two more babies have been born and were helped into this world as skilfully as always by your dear mother. One of these days, you will be delivering the babies of tenants on the land of your Gentleman husband and they will be very fortunate."

"Oh no, Goodwife Wright, I don't want to leave The Manor - ever. How could I when there are so many people who I love dearly right here."

"And we love you, too, Mistress Margory. But when you fall in love with a Gentleman, you will want to be mistress of his home and land."

"No, Goodwife Wright, you're wrong. I don't ever want to leave here, so let's say no more about it."

I had spoken a little more crisply to Goodwife Wright than I usually did, but the idea of leaving Arthur behind was unthinkable. There, I had admitted it again. I believed that I was beginning to give my heart to Arthur. Did he feel the same way? And would mother and father allow such a relationship? Certainly, mother would not be at all happy about it, but what would father think?

Chapter 42

The meal that day was the first time I would be seeing Arthur since my return; I must be careful not to show my feelings or dress inappropriately. My parents and I had had our game soup served when the servants came in and sat at the other end of the dining table. I glanced towards them, but there was no returning acknowledgement from Arthur. He seemed, instead, to be engrossed in conversation with the new servant, Lucy, and my maid, Hannah. I noticed that he had sat down between them again. Had he always sat next to them and I just hadn't noticed where everyone else was sitting? The only person I had ever noticed at the servants' end of the table was Arthur. It was as though a large spotlight played on him, leaving everyone else in the dark and he, the only one I could see.

Oh, there now. Finally, he had stopped talking to Hannah for a moment and seemed to remember my presence. He smiled that wonderfully warm smile and I inclined my head very slightly. I would not return his smile, as had been my habit. He must learn that I would not allow him to smile at me and then return to speaking to a pretty maid. I must be the only one to whom he gave all his attention. Was that father who had addressed me?

"Darling, I'm going into London today and thought you might like to go with me. I shall be there today and tomorrow and staying overnight for just one night. I shall be meeting some important people, with whom we shall be dining this evening, so mother will help you to choose an appropriate dress. She tells me that you bought several in Gloucester. We shall be leaving within the hour, so I would like you to pack right away as the horses will be brought for us at two of the clock."

Father had never taken me to London before. This must be mother's wish, once again, to separate me from Arthur and in the hope of my meeting a Gentleman. I glanced towards him but he was deep in conversation with the two servants again. Walking the length of the table, I ignored both Arthur and Lucy and said,

"Hannah. Quickly, I need you to pack for a night's stay in London."

Not used to hearing the sharp edge in my voice, Hannah quickly left Arthur mid-sentence, I noticed, and scurried up the staircase. I would need to keep an eye on that girl. In my bedchamber, I looked at her afresh. Yes, she was much too pretty for my liking. Her nose was small and her big, darkly lashed eyes were an unusual shade of violet. Why hadn't I noticed that before? And young, of course. Hannah was only 12. Yes, I would need to be careful that Arthur's smile and conversation were not given to Hannah too often. This would require thought.

Hannah had started to lay out my purple taffeta dress when I addressed her.

"Please make sure that you put out everything I shall need in London, including a few of my less expensive jewels. While I'm away, I would like you to put my dresses in order as well as taking everything out of my drawers and cleaning them. I shall be accompanied by mother's maid, Beatrice, because she has had experience of London society which you have not. So mother will want you to be her acting maid while I'm away. Mother is very particular so you will need to make sure that she has everything she needs while Beatrice is away. You will need to work hard and not be inclined to do other activities. While you are laying out my best riding habit, I must speak to father. If you're not sure about any aspect of my dress, hair or lipsticks, just ask Beatrice. Also be sure to pack my favourite comb and mirror."

"Yes, Mistress Margory" she replied demurely, dropping a curtsey.

Finally, our best horses were ready and longing to be leaving. Father had told four of the groomsmen in addition to his manservant, Stephen, to accompany us as the ride into London was much more perilous than that to Gloucester. I felt rather nervous at the prospect, but excited, too. Father would take good care of me and the grooms had been part of our household for a very long time. They often accompanied father into London so I had little reason for concern. Also, the monarch rode this highway so it was kept in good repair.

Chapter 43

Eventually we left, with mother waving to us and all the household, including Hannah, Lucy and Arthur standing together at the great door of The Manor. I noticed again how pretty these two girls were, and pushed the thought aside. Arthur didn't yet know it, but he would be mine. I did wish that he wouldn't stand so close to Hannah, though. A little worry-worm awoke in me.

Out on the open highway, though, that worm was blown away by the wind in the trees, the sound of the bubbling streams and occasional calls of voices and birdsong. The birds were full of mirth, joy and cheeriness and the ripples in the stream gurgled merrily in accompaniment. I felt very happy to be a wealthy young woman with loving parents who would soon be seeing their daughter married. Nothing was going to stand in the way of my love for Arthur – for I was sure this was how true love felt – and our life would be wonderful. Perhaps I would plant a seed in father's mind while we were in London, but for now, I would ride like the wind. Father reminded me,

"Remember, my dear, that, as we draw nearer to London, we shall see many gallows, with criminals hanging from the ropes. The men will ride close to you at these times so that you will see as little as possible. Although they are a dreadful sight, I want you to remember that they are there because they have committed evil acts and this is their punishment. Also, I suggest that you cover your nose and avert your gaze when we ride by. These men will not only have been there for some time, but they will not be wearing any clothes. The stench is often putrid."

I gasped at the thought, having never seen anyone else naked. I would do as father said and look away. I would be very pleased to see the bustle of the streets of London, although I would miss the fresh smelling countryside that I was used to in my daily life. London was said to be very exciting, but father always said that it was certainly not fresh smelling! I had heard tell of the centre of the city itself, where the houses were so crowded that people could lean out of one and reach the hand of the person living opposite. Many people, I knew, lived on the only bridge, called London Bridge, that had many stone arches through which ships could sail. I knew that people often moved around London by the River Thames and that many streets had steps down to the river. But I knew so little about it, really, that I couldn't wait to see more.

Eventually, we stopped at The White Hart in Drury Lane that I had been told was very fashionable; it was there we were to dine and the horses could be fed and watered. My father immediately took charge,

"Boy! Take our horses. Make them ready for our return journey tomorrow."

So while the horses were unsaddled to take to the stables at the rear, the ostler took our bags and led us to the Innkeeper. Father asked for his usual, large rooms, my own containing a truckle bed for Beatrice. While father conducted his meetings, Beatrice unpacked my gowns. Father had insisted that I was not to take many jewels with me, for fear of theft, so, instead, I'd told

Harriet to pack a dress that was sewn with strands of silver. A bath had been brought into the room and Beatrice was filling it from large jugs. I had also told Hannah to put rose petals, spices and herbs in my cases and Beatrice now added those to my bath water.

Father had arranged for us to dine in his fine chamber as much feasting was taking place in the hall. When I joined him at dinner, I knew that I looked my best in my purple gown. I did so want to speak privately to him, away from mother's ears. Imagine my surprise and disappointment, therefore, when I saw that he had asked two young men to join us and, although they were certainly Gentlemen, they were not as handsome as my Arthur.

"May I introduce you to my dear daughter, Margory."

"Margory, this is Andrew, the son of Lord Entwhistle, and this is Henry, the son of Sir Percival Sarratt."

I dipped a curtsey but couldn't help noticing that, although they were very well mannered, their faces showed a trace of disappointment. It looked as though father had perhaps been a little generous in my description. But father was still speaking.

"Margory is, of course, my only child, and will inherit my entire estate in Hertfordshire. Some young man will be very fortunate."

I blushed at these words. I suspected that the young men before me would prefer to be seen walking out with a pretty, young woman of few resources rather than a plain, rich one. Dear father. I loved him so. He was probably the only man in the world who thought that he had a handsome daughter. But I was the fortunate one. It would not suit my case to have one of these men falling in love with me when my heart lay elsewhere. So I smiled graciously and told them how very pleased I was to meet them. No one knew, of course, that I intended to have Arthur. Whether mother approved or not.

After we had washed our hands, several servants brought out a number of delicious dishes, including fresh, fat river eels in butter sauce, roasted curlew and, finally, two types of cheese – Dutch and Cheshire. But the two young Gentlemen did not linger long. So it was only a short time later that I found myself alone with father - exactly as I had planned. He patted my hand.

"When we return, I shall speak to your mother about giving a ball, to which Andrew and Henry will be invited and anyone else she considers to be suitable. Time is passing quickly and I would like to see you settled in your own manor house, surrounded by your own family, God willing."

This was my moment, and I did not intend to lose it.

"May I speak to you about a subject that has been on my mind for some time, father?"

"Of course, my child. What is it?"

Chapter 44

On our return journey the following day, I sighed with contentment. My soaring heart was not even to be dampened by the dreadful sights at the crossroads, even when I heard one of the groomsmen shout,

"Ten hanging men ahead!"

Finally, we were home. At the sound of our horses' hooves, mother came out to greet us, embracing first father then me so tightly I thought she would never let us go. The servants, meanwhile, had gathered, too. I glanced quickly at Hannah who seemed to be looking particularly pleased with herself. Was that a small smile I saw before she dipped her head?

"Thank you, Lord", my mother whispered, "for bringing my dearest family home to me safely. Have you had a nice time, darling? Did you meet some amiable Gentlemen?"

She beamed as I confirmed that they were, indeed, very amiable.

"Hannah, unpack Mistress Margory's cases and prepare a bath. I shall tell the Housekeeper that we shall be taking tea in an hour."

And turning back to me,

"I've asked cook to make your favourite cake. You're looking so beautifully slender now, you deserve a reward. I want to hear all about your excursion to London."

Chapter 45

Climbing the wide staircase to my room, I closed the door behind me. I needed to know what had been happening while I was away; my worry-worm began to stir again.

"Have you taken good care of Lady Francis's needs while I was away, Hannah?"

"Oh yes, Mistress Margory. I helped whenever I could. The Mistress was very considerate, too, and allowed me to have yesterday afternoon free to, er, do as I wished."

Noticing her hesitation, and trying not to look too alarmed, I asked,

"Oh yes, and what did you do?"

Speaking so quietly I could barely hear her, she said,

"I went for a very long walk in the beautiful sunshine and found a place I liked in the woods."

Not MY place, I hoped inwardly.

"Speak up, Hannah. Were you alone in your walk?"

My own annoyance was beginning to meet her heightening distress at my tone of voice and I repeated,

"And did you take this walk alone?"

"I didn't think the Mistress would want me to walk alone, so I was pleased when the Master's manservant suggested he should accompany me."

In spite of her trembling voice, my heart missed a beat.

"Let me see, his name is Arthur, isn't it? Do you mean that you went for a long walk into the woods with Arthur?"

Hannah began to pant a little, and speaking very quickly said,

"Yes, but I asked for Mistress's permission and she said that was perfectly satisfactory. I did ask her first. In fact, Mistress Margory, she seemed very pleased. I told her that we have taken several walks that way in recent times. I have told Lucy each time, so that if I were to be needed at The Manor, she would immediately come to tell me. Her Ladyship said that was perfectly satisfactory."

She looked at me expectantly.

Yes, I thought, my mother would have been very pleased indeed at this turn of events. I swallowed my growing trepidation, trying to brush it aside.

"Wash my back, Hannah, and be sure to use the soap I like, the one with rose perfume."

"I've got it here, ready for you, Mistress. I know how much you like it."

Mother had always commented that I tended to be a little clumsy, and this seemed to be increased by my annoyance at her news. It was then that, to my horror, the wet, slippery soap suddenly seemed to gain a life of its own. It sprang out of my hands onto the floor, just as Hannah was moving around to the other side of the bath. The whole scene seemed to slow before my eyes as Hannah fell, one leg twisted under her body. My annoyance dissipated as quickly as a popped balloon as her scream brought mother rushing into the bedchamber.

"What happened? Oh, poor Hannah. Can you stand? And why is there so much blood?"

Sadly, Hannah could not stand at all; as for the blood, I assumed she had struck something sharp when she had fallen. What else could it have been?

A groom was sent immediately to our family surgeon who lived nearby. He said that Hannah's leg was broken and she must rest for several weeks; he would then visit again to see how it was getting on. I noticed that he took my mother aside, telling her something in a low voice, at which she looked shocked, but quickly regained her composure as Hannah whispered,

"But I told someone that I would walk with him later today."

In spite of my earlier feelings of annoyance regarding Hannah and Arthur walking out together, I felt truly sorry about Hannah's accident. However, I had to admit to feeling relieved that this walking together would not be taking place for some time now. Looking at her sympathetically, I said

"I'm sorry to say that, once you have taken to your bed, you won't be walking with anyone for quite some time, Hannah. You must stay there until the surgeon says that you are well enough to start walking a little again. I shall ask mother if one of the other servants can stay with you because we must make sure that you don't do anything you shouldn't. You seem to have befriended Lucy, so I shall speak to her myself. I shall arrange for you both to have a bedchamber on this floor, instead of with the other servants downstairs. There, won't you like that? You won't be lonely while Lucy is with you. In that way, Lady Francis and I will know that you are resting all day and all night. If you need anything at all, Lucy will let me know immediately."

Mother, who had been listening to what I had to say, had begun with a perplexed shaking of her head, but was now nodding.

"Hannah, that is very generous of Mistress Margory as she needs her maids every day. It is important that you rest so that your bones can mend and recover. This has been a very sad accident."

I truly felt sorry for Hannah's pain. At the same time, I couldn't deceive myself into thinking that I felt unhappy that she would not be walking with Arthur for some time. That made me very happy indeed.

Chapter 46

Eating a little cake with mother, later, I began to relax.

"Margory, my dear, you look better than I've seen you looking for some considerable time. It can't be the dreadful London air, so it must be that you enjoyed the company of one of the young Gentlemen in Gloucester, in particular. Now do tell me, which one was he? Was it the one I mentioned?"

I did, indeed, feel very well. With Hannah unable to go for walks with Arthur, the way was clear to put my plan into action. Also, my ensuring that Lucy was no longer a part of Arthur's daily life either was an added advantage. I smiled, and, in case my mother's perceptive eye should wonder why, I said,

"Mother. My favourite cake tasted particularly delicious today so, with your permission, I shall go and thank cook personally. I shall then go to Hannah to ensure that she has everything she needs and is not tempted to put even one toe out of bed. I shall also make sure that Lucy has moved her belongings to the bed next to Hannah so that she is able to keep her company and watch her at all times."

Was that a brief look of suspicion that crossed my dear mother's face? If so, it was quickly replaced by her usual, gentle demeanour.

"What a sweet girl you are, Margory."

Father, meanwhile, was away again, on some sort of local political business, and had taken Stephen with him, for probably the last time. He had said that the changes wrought by Edward VI, with the help of his advisors, to the Roman Catholic church and the country, were now being reversed by Mary. And certainly, I knew that in our own church of St Giles, the colourful stained glass windows had been changed to plain and the services were conducted in English instead of Latin. It was so confusing, and I didn't like the changes either. However, father said I mustn't talk about it, although he was very unhappy about them, too. When he returned from these discussions, he always looked very tired and was beginning to look older than his years, I thought.

However, in spite of father's absence, that evening, the dining table resumed its previous pleasure, with mother and me talking at one end. I allowed myself a glance at Arthur on one occasion and hoped that wasn't disappointment I saw on his face. I looked away quickly without acknowledging his smile and focused on mother's words. I wouldn't look in his direction again this evening. He must be made aware that mine was the only face he should look upon.

The following morning, I went down to the kitchen, at a time I knew most of the servants would be there, and told them,

"As you know, Hannah had the most dreadful fall yesterday. Mother generously sent for our own personal, family surgeon who has stipulated specifically that she must be left alone to rest. I have therefore asked Lucy to stay with her, and I shall have to manage with fewer maids. I know that you wish her well, and I shall tell her so. If you would like her to receive any special messages, I would like you to bring them to me and I shall pass them on, as I need to make sure that she doesn't become over-excited. I shall be visiting Hannah as often as I can. The surgeon has said that, on no account must she get out of bed until he visits her again in six weeks' time. So, of course, that means that she must not walk at all. I'm sure you all understand that, as you, like me, want her to recover as quickly as possible. If she does try to walk, the surgeon has said that she will be left with a permanent limp, and none of us want that to happen, do we."

Joining mother for breakfast, I asked when father would be returning.

"In about four days, my dear. In the meantime, you and I can start planning the ball, to which we shall invite Charles, Henry, Peter and Andrew. I shall also send a letter to your aunt Juliana to see if Robert and Cecil are free as they could bring one or two of their friends whom you met in Gloucester."

"I think that father has one or two other young Gentlemen in mind, too, as well as Sir William Garrard's sons and daughter, Anne, who I met at my Confirmation. So perhaps we should wait until he returns before the guest list is finalised. We don't, after all, want to miss out anyone important."

Mother's reaction was instantaneous,

"My dear girl, I am delighted that you are showing such an interest in the ball. As Sir William is now Lord Mayor of London, it will be good for the county to see that he is a family friend. I have always been sorry that you are an only child, with only the tenants' children to play with and talk to. Most of them are, of course, well behaved, pleasant young people. However, they have not been fortunate enough to be the sons and daughters of a Gentleman and so they are very different from you. I couldn't be happier that you are now meeting suitable young men."

I said nothing.

The following day, before mother could start speaking to me once again about my superior position in society, about which I just could not agree, I decided to take a ride on my favourite horse, Chestnut.

"Enjoy your ride, darling, and make sure you're back for our meal. Shall I ask one of the grooms to ride with you? I don't like you to be on your own in case something should happen. I couldn't bear the thought of you lying somewhere, injured."

"I'll take extra care, mother, just for you."

"What a dear, sweet girl you are. Why would I want more than one child when you are the embodiment of everything that is special in a daughter."

I was very pleased that mother was expressing such loving thoughts towards me as they may not last long when my plan was put into action. And, of course, she would not know that it had been MY suggestion to father. As a dutiful daughter, I was perfectly happy to agree to whatever father suggested. But in spite of loving my mother dearly, I just could not agree with her about the lack of interweaving between classes.

But those were four very long, tedious days awaiting father's return. I read, I rode, I completed my diary, I sewed and continued my tapestry as well as discussing plans for the ball with mother. The late autumn leaves burnished bronze, brown and orange and

I enjoyed walking through the knot garden and kitchen garden, on to the fields and woods. And, of course, I visited Hannah and had told mother,

"I think I shall read to poor Hannah from the new Bible. She doesn't read, of course, and it would help to pass the time for her, as well as giving her something to think about. I may begin with the Ten Commandments, to show her what a Godly household she lives in and is fortunate to be a part of."

"That's a very good and very thoughtful idea, Margory. Why don't you go and speak to Hannah about that now. As well as looking so well, darling, I think that a kindness is beginning to show in you that has sometimes not been very evident in the past. I'm very happy to see that you are becoming such a fine, sensible young woman who is almost ready to manage a large household such as we have here at The Manor. I do look forward to that day and to you having your very own family."

Finally, mother and I were beginning to think the same things, although she wasn't to know, of course, that I already had a husband in mind.

Chapter 47

Walking into the bedroom now occupied by Hannah, I said,

"That will be all, Lucy. You can speak to the housekeeper to see where you can help in the house. Come back in two hours' time to resume your place with Hannah." Then, turning to Hannah who looked pale, I said,

"How are you feeling today, Hannah? It's such a shame that you can't move from this room. Do you have everything you want? I've decided that I'm going to spoil you during this time of your not being able to walk at all. Which are your favourite sweetmeats? Tell me which foods you particularly like and you shall have them in abundance."

"Please, Mistress Margory, I don't..."

"No, no, I won't accept any of your remonstrances, I shall speak to cook this very day. Yes, I see that perhaps you are becoming a little heavier, but you must enjoy yourself as much as you can during these six weeks.

Now, I don't think you read, do you?"

A slow shaking of the head met my question.

"No, I thought not. In that case, I shall read to you from the Bible. My family, of course, has its own copy, so I can't give it to you, much as I would like to. Bibles are not given to people such as yourself, as you probably know. Even we high-born ladies must read it in private. Mother was only saying this morning that we are all born into different levels of society and that we must remember which part of society we belong to. Here at The Manor, we are very wealthy, of course, and we are perfectly happy to help the poor around us, such as yourself. I hope that you realise that?"

Hannah looked at me so sadly that I suddenly felt very sorry indeed about her accident. The poor girl. How I would hate to have to lie still for six weeks. My heart went out to her and I patted her hand. At that, I saw tears begin to flow as she said softly,

"Oh yes, Mistress, I do know my place. I hope that I haven't done anything to offend you? I thought perhaps I had?"

Recovering my composure, I said,

"Hannah. How can you think such a thing when my family and I have provided you with everything you want and need since your fall. Our own family surgeon was sent for immediately, I have asked Lucy to remain with you as much as her other duties will allow and I am visiting you as often as I can. And now I am suggesting that I, personally, read to you. I hope you're not an ungrateful girl!"

"Oh no, Mistress Margory, please don't say that. I'm not at all ungrateful. Although...".

"Yes?"

"While I like Lucy very much, I am lonely here, in this bed, in this bedchamber every day. Will you allow me to have some other visitors? Some of the other servants?"

This was not, of course, something I would allow as on no account must Arthur visit Hannah. Particularly in the bedroom where Hannah looked, not only pretty, but very vulnerable. Oh, no, I couldn't allow that, so I told her,

"I thought you were grateful, Hannah, and here you are suggesting something that is contrary to the surgeon's wishes. He particularly said that you must rest and not become agitated. Are you asking me to go against his wishes? Because that is something that neither mother nor I can allow. Now, today, I shall begin by reading the Bible to you."

Chapter 48

Finally, it was the day of father's return. I felt both very excited and very calm. What would father say, and when would he say it? He was, of course, head of our household and whatever he decided was carried out. Naturally, if it was something with which mother disagreed strongly, then father would listen and it would be discussed. However, if father felt strongly, too, then it was his word that was followed. I was so happy to see him again and to have a livelier discussion at our dinner table that evening. At the same time, I was relieved when our meal came to an end, with father saying to mother,

"My dear, I would like you to join me in the library as there is a matter I wish to discuss with you. Margory, I know that you wish to continue with your book, so I suggest that you do that in one of the withdrawing rooms."

I nodded dutifully.

Later, when they had emerged from the library, and after kissing them goodnight, I said that I would retire early. I noticed that mother looked very annoyed and father, determined. It looked likely that father had suggested my plan to mother.

The following day dawned sunny and bright so I decided to take out Chestnut again as he did so enjoy our ride across the land. I had got the impression from father the previous evening that the smaller landowners were beginning to experience a little financial difficulty. As a result, they were considering enclosing some of their land and turning it into pasture for sheep, as wool was paying well. That meant ending tenancies, which father said he, himself, definitely did not want to do. Not at the moment anyway. Mother said that she would visit our tenants in the coming weeks in order to reassure them that there were no plans to do that on our land. I had said that I would go with her to talk to the older children. But, for now, I would enjoy the light breeze in my long hair riding Chestnut.

Chapter 49

That evening, I dressed with care, making sure that the dress I wore was one of my simpler ones. As time went on, I could be a little more adventurous.

Father was just about to be seated at the dining table, but Arthur was already there. A place had been set for him at my family's end of the table. I thought he looked a little nervous and the other servants were staring and muttering.

As I approached the table, I heard bits of whisperings,

"What's he doing down that end?"

"He's been thinking he's better than he is for a long time."

"We know whose idea that is, don't we!"

"Don't understand. Surprised Lady Francis has allowed that."

"Maybe he doesn't like sitting with us."

Father spoke loudly, over-riding the gossip.

"Good evening, Arthur."

Arthur stood.

"Good evening, Sir."

"I shall say Grace when her Ladyship has joined us."

"Yes, Sir."

"Good evening, Arthur."

Arthur stood for a second time.

"Good evening, Mistress Margory."

"Good evening, Arthur."

My mother's words were spiked with ice,

Arthur stood a third time, looking even more

nervous at the entrance of mother.

"Good evening, Lady Francis."

My mother's three words were among the very few she spoke for some time, with father conducting an almost one-way conversation.

"How beautifully sunny it is today."

"Yes dear."

"We are fortunate that it will be much cooler here in the country than in London."

"Yes, dear."

"Sir William Garrard has boundless energy in helping the poor. I admire that man immensely."

Still, mother continued to concentrate on her meal, rarely glancing at anyone.

Father was becoming a little irritated, I could see.

"Arthur. I invited you to join my family for our two main meals of the day because I'm very pleased indeed with your progress since becoming one of my manservants. You have shown intelligence, discretion, tact and consideration in pursuing your duties and I am very pleased with you. You show an aptitude for learning that I am delighted to see. Joining my family at these meal times will further that learning as you will discover the manners of the Gentry. You will, of course, continue to join the other servants to break your fast each morning. My main manservant, Stephen, is now becoming rather frail and I would like to think that you will take over from him, when the time is right."

"I'm very grateful for your generosity, sir".

"Good. There will be a great deal for you to absorb but I have total confidence in your ability to do it. The change from, say, wooden plates and bowls to silver or pewter concerns me not a jot, and I'm sure you will enjoy the different sorts of food my family is used to. I suggest that you adapt to these sorts of things in the same, quick way you have already shown".

"Thank you very much, sir. I appreciate the opportunity you are giving me."

"And so you should."

Mother's patience had held long enough and she clearly didn't intend to hide her dissatisfaction any longer. But neither did father intend to tread a negative path regarding his decision.

"Yes, my dear, and I think he does. If you continue to do well, Arthur, there will be other rewards."

Mother's questioning look was met with a smile. But all I could think was what a dear, dear father I had. I would look forward to each and every main meal now, knowing that I would be sitting across the table from that handsome face and wondrous smile. This was one of the happiest days of my life, and I was sure there would be many more.

* * *

Dear Diary,

The hand that writes this evening is indeed a very happy hand. Father has most kindly acquiesced to my suggestion of telling Arthur to join our family for the two meals each day. I knew that father was very happy with the way he has carried out his duties and has wanted to reward him in some way other than financial. So, in fact, when I spoke to father about my idea in London, it was something that he had himself been considering. At the end of our discussion, it was clear that this was father's idea, not my own, and that made me very happy. It also meant that father would be better placed to persuade mother, although I suspect that that was not very easy. However, father is a clever man. What my father did not say, as it would have been rather indelicate, is that, although he loves me very much, he is disappointed not to have had a son to inherit his estate. While Arthur is not that son, he is a young man whom father likes and trusts and wants to encourage to make more of himself; father can help him to do that. Of course, mother is aware of this disappointment and would not have discouraged him as vigorously as she might, had the family situation been different. However, that is not to say she is pleased about Arthur joining us at the meal table. It simply means that she must accept it.

Chapter 50

And so it was. Arthur began to join my parents and me at the head of our very long dining table. On that first, wonderful day, and having said grace, father looked up,

"Welcome to joining my family at meal times, Arthur. For a boy of your age, you are the best manservant I have ever had. Although you have not been with me very long, you have learned your duties very well. You are an intelligent boy and a fast learner. You are totally reliable, and I am happy to reward you by giving you a seat at our meal table. As Stephen knows, he will, of course be retiring soon and I shall consider your taking his place, should your improvement continue. Would you like that?"

"I would like that very much, Sir, and shall do everything I can to help you in your daily activities."

"I'm very pleased to hear that, Arthur. There is one other thing that I haven't mentioned to either you or my dear daughter."

I raised my eyes and glanced at mother questioningly. But she appeared also to be wondering what father was about to say.

"Mistress Margory does, of course, know how to read, write and to do arithmetic, and, in order for you to be of particular help to me, I would like her to teach you, too. We are also privileged, naturally, to have our own Bible, and this will be included in your studies, when appropriate. My daughter has known you most of your life and I don't think there is a better person to undertake such a task."

I lowered my eyes lest they show as orbs of gratitude, and as mother turned to gaze at me questioningly.

"Perhaps I should have spoken to Margory first before speaking to you of this, Arthur. Do you have any objection to teaching Arthur these subjects, Margory? I am happy to hear if you do not think this is something you would be prepared to do."

Before I could reply, mother could contain herself no longer.

"My dear. Of course you know best, but is this really necessary? None of the other servants read or write, and neither do any of Arthur's family. We don't want to embarrass Arthur among people of his own kind."

"I think we should leave that to Arthur, my dear. What do you think, m'boy? Will this learning drive a stake between you and your fellow servants, or between you and your family?"

"With your permission, Sir, I shall speak to my family today, but I'm sure that they will be very pleased indeed that you are honouring me in this way; they respect your judgement very much. And if any of the other servants are not happy with your generosity, well, I shall have to hope that they will grow to understand why you have made this offer."

He said this with such conviction and courage that even I was surprised, and I could see that mother was, too. Arthur was proving already to be more than a handsome face. I, for one, could barely contain my impatience to start teaching him. What a wonderful surprise. Father had not only rewarded Arthur, he had made me extremely happy, too, and my face shone with delight.

"I shall go to the library right away and draw up a schedule of lessons. With your permission, father, when Arthur has spoken to his parents, I shall speak to him again, tomorrow afternoon to ensure that the lessons are at a time that fit in with his duties to you."

"An excellent idea, Margory. Don't you think so, my dear?"

Mother mumbled something that was so indistinct, I don't think anyone heard what she was trying to say. Collecting herself, she said,

"I now have to speak to cook and the housekeeper about the ball we shall be giving. It is only two weeks away and there is a great deal to be arranged. All the servants will have extra duties, so your lessons with Arthur will have to take second place, Margory. He will have many additional duties to carry out for your father."

"Whatever you say, mother. In the meantime, I shall go to the library now, and start planning the schedule. I shall see you in the library at 3 of the clock tomorrow, Arthur, once you have spoken to your family."

"Of course," father continued, "I shall have Stephen for a few months more, so this will certainly be an ideal time for Arthur to begin his extra learning."

"And I shall do whatever you think I need to do, mother, in helping to arrange the ball."

Now that things were turning out even better than I'd hoped, I needed to take extra care to ensure that I did everything I could to please mother. After all, this had been quite a shock for her and I didn't think for one moment that I had heard the last of it. Mother had always been very perceptive, and she didn't lose any time in expressing her feelings when we were alone.

"Did you know of father's plans for Arthur before today, Margory? It seems to have happened very suddenly and was certainly a surprise for me. Were you surprised, too?"

I hesitated. This called for my slight side-stepping.

"Dear mother, I thought father would have discussed with you first the possibility of Arthur joining us for our two main meals. Surely he did that?"

"Naturally, of course he did. But I knew nothing of the plan to educate Arthur in reading, writing and arithmetic. Nor that he would ask you to undertake the task. Did you know anything of that?"

I was relieved to be able to answer that totally sincerely.

"I was as surprised as you were, mother, when father made that suggestion. However, on reflection, I do think it's a good idea, don't you, as Stephen knows nothing of these subjects. It will be very helpful for father to have a manservant who is able to help him even more than dear old Stephen does. And, think of it, mother. We shall be the first in the county to have an educated manservant. You will be greatly admired for having such a modern household."

I glanced at mother's face and was delighted to see her shoulders straighten and her head lift, proudly. Mother's pride was always very easy to tap into.

"You are quite right, my dear. I shall make it clear to those Ladies of my acquaintance that no money is being spent on this education. We are fortunate to have a daughter who is able to pass on the skills. Yes, you are quite right, this is something that will set our household apart as being a little superior to others in the county. I shall speak to cook and the other servants now and shall ensure that they realise what an enlightened household they serve. It is market day in Greenwillows tomorrow which will be an ideal time for the servants to spread the word, too. Off you go now and start planning your lessons."

I gave an inward sigh of relief. Mother didn't realise that my long-term plan went well beyond Arthur's education.

"Yes, mother. I shall do that right away – unless, of course, there's anything I can help you with first?"

"No, no, child. The sooner you start your plans, the quicker word will be spread. I shall see you later this evening."

How pleased I was! From now on, I would not only be seeing Arthur opposite me for our two meals of the day, but also would be spending time teaching him. And we would be alone at that time. Just the two of us. My happiness knew no bounds and I immediately went and sat at my desk in the library – my favourite room – to plan his lessons. I knew very well that he would be a quick learner, so ensuring that these lessons would not be short-lived would not be easy. But after all, in order to learn properly, one must take one's time and I did want to teach Arthur properly.

Chapter 51

"Mistress Margory, Hannah is asking to see you."

So lost was I in my preparations that I hadn't heard Lucy's soft knock on the library door.

"Please tell her that I shall come along presently, but that I am very busy with important business at the moment. Take her one of cook's special cakes. I have asked you, Lucy, to take care of Hannah."

"Yes, Mistress, but she did sound rather alarmed."

I felt so happy that I could not bring a glare to my face, but it sufficed to simply look up and stare at Lucy for a moment. I certainly did not intend to be interrupted by small matters. Had Hannah not begun to try to take my place in Arthur's affections? Me, the daughter of the house. I must have another talk to her about the place of servants in a wealthy household. Still holding Lucy's gaze, I said,

"I hope I am correct in thinking that you are not arguing with me, Lucy, are you? Do as I say and tell Hannah that I shall visit her when I can. Away with you, girl."

"Yes, Mistress, I shall do that right away."

As I began to break away my stare from Lucy's face, she turned quickly and gave an exclamation of pain. Was she now walking away with a limp that I hadn't noticed when she had entered the library? How strange. Perhaps the girl suffered from some sort of arthritis, like her mother, about which we were beginning to know just a little. However, I certainly did not have time to consider anyone except Arthur at the moment.

But a few moments later, there was yet another knock at the door. I sighed in frustration,

"Come."

"Mistress Margory."

"Yes, what is it?"

Would I never be allowed to work without interruption? This time, it was cook.

"I'm sorry to disturb you, Mistress Margory, but Lucy has just come to me, asking for a cake for Hannah. This will be her fifth this week and I am concerned that she is growing fat."

Oh my, a fat Hannah. That had indeed not crossed my mind. Just as I was becoming increasingly slender, Hannah was gaining in body weight. Oh dear. What a shame.

"Cook. Let me make this clear. Hannah is ill. My parents gave permission for our very own, private surgeon to visit her and he particularly said that she must rest. Not only have I arranged for Lucy to be her constant companion, I have ensured that she has no visitors, as the surgeon stipulated she must not be agitated. I, myself, have visited her regularly and want to make sure that she has special sweetmeats to help pass her tedious day. Perhaps you have not been told that I am reading to Hannah from my family's very own Bible – something that I need not do, under the circumstances, but have chosen to do. Now, do you not think she is an extremely fortunate young woman to have so much attention given to her? And now, if I hear you correctly, you are suggesting that I should withdraw part of my kindness. Please do as I ordered and give a particularly delicious sweetmeat to Lucy so that she can give it to Hannah. In the meantime, would you please tell the servants that I am very busy and do not wish to be disturbed, under any circumstances." I finished this request rather sternly, so that cook was fully aware of my seriousness on the subject.

As she waddled away, Cook closed the door quietly behind her. Really, I could not be expected to conduct teaching sessions as well as running up and down, to tend to a servant. That was exactly why I had asked Lucy to be with Hannah in the bedchamber. I certainly did not have the time to be consulted about such things as cakes for Hannah when I had important teaching to plan.

Chapter 52

Arthur didn't join us at the dining table the following mid-day as he was speaking to his parents, brothers and sisters about his new position at The Manor.

At 3 of the clock I heard the longed-for knock on the door. I was surprised how confident a knock it was, so I took a little time in neatening my dress and bringing the chair in which he would be sitting a little closer to my desk. Although I knew that my feelings for Arthur were growing, I must not forget my position, as mother had pointed out, and neither must Arthur forget his. I waited just a moment longer until I heard a second, softer knock. Yes, that was more appropriate.

"Enter."

How handsome Arthur looked. I had not seen him since our meal the previous evening. Such a short time, yet how my heart had looked forward to seeing him. His pale, shoulder-length hair was neatly combed, he had put on a clean, smart uniform and his shoes shone, as did his eyes. As he would need to always look extremely clean and smart, I must buy a special ivory or horn comb for him as he probably combed his wonderful locks with the wooden lice comb used by the rest of his family; I thought vaguely that I was glad he did not appear to require an ear scoop, too. Yes, he must begin to look like the Gentleman I knew he would become – but only with my help, of course.

"Come in, Arthur, and sit on this chair, next to me, so that we can look at these exercises together. We are going to start with the alphabet that is used for reading and writing."

"Begging your pardon, Mistress Margory, but I have always been interested in figures and I would like to start with arithmetic first. I'm very eager to learn arithmetic so that I can begin to help Stephen and Master with the Master's bills as soon as possible."

"Yes, and we shall deal with arithmetic when I am ready to do so, Arthur. I do hope that you will keep in mind the generosity shown by both my father and me. Father has given you a place with his very own, dear family, at the head of the table, so that you can join us for our main meals. He has done this with not a little difficulty in persuading my mother that it would be a good idea. In addition to that, he is giving you the privilege of being taught reading, writing and arithmetic by me and, again, this is something that I hope you appreciate as being very unusual for a person of your status. I have spent part of today preparing your first lesson in writing and now you are suggesting that I have wasted my time because what YOU want is to learn arithmetic. I had not thought it would be necessary, Arthur, for me to point out that this is not what you WANT, but what is GOOD for you. Perhaps you don't realise, Arthur, how very fortunate you are to be the only student here and being taught by the daughter of the house. If you were to attend school in London, you would be one of many, with all classes being taught in the same room. Not only that, the master sits with a book in one hand and a birch in the other, I'm told."

I then moved the chair a little further away from my desk. Mother was quite right. Arthur's background was very different from my own and he must learn that I was superior and he was inferior. That must be made very clear from the outset.

I believe I saw a moment of surprise cross Arthur's face, but it didn't linger, and was immediately replaced by the beautiful smile that I loved so much. Good. Arthur was already learning.

* * *

I needn't have worried. Arthur learned his lessons very well, lapping them up like the thirstiest of kittens. That pleased me as I loved kittens. Soon, he was starting to read the Bible, beginning with the 10 Commandments, which I explained in great detail, particularly as they related to my own parents. I was also going to be reading the Bible to Hannah, although, of course, she could not read and would never read. I certainly didn't want a shared interest to bring these two together even more.

As though my thoughts had circulated the whole house, there was a rather urgent-sounding knock at the library door.

Wearily, I told whoever it was to enter.

"I have given instructions that I am not to be disturbed between 3 and 4 of the clock in the afternoon."

It was Lucy, Hannah's companion, yet again, whose expression softened, I noticed, when she glanced swiftly at Arthur. Did these servants not realise that he belonged to me, and me alone?

"Yes, what is it, Lucy? Surely it can wait until I have completed my teaching for the day."

"Mistress Margory, I am indeed very sorry to disturb you yet again, but I hope you know that I would not do so unless the matter was of an urgent nature. It concerns Hannah."

I noticed Arthur's head snap up before, once more, resuming his place in the Bible.

"Mistress Margory, Hannah is very hot indeed and could not sleep last night for tossing and turning. This morning she looked at me as though she didn't know me and was mumbling strangely. I feel afraid, Mistress, because this is what happened to my mother..."

This was indeed unexpected, but Arthur had only just started his class for the day and I was certainly not going to be parted from him until the full hour had elapsed.

"Yes, yes, Lucy. I haven't got time to consider your mother's illness. Has anyone been visiting Hannah? I explicitly gave instructions that she should not be agitated."

"No, Mistress, they have not, and I am with her throughout the day and night, so I would know, had she been distressed by anyone or anything."

"Very well. Return immediately to Hannah, and I'll visit her as soon as I can, but it will not be in less than an hour."

"As you wish, Mistress."

I could not help but see that Lucy's shoulders had drooped as she turned away and, yes, she was now most certainly walking with a limp. How curious. The library door was closed softly and I breathed a sigh of relief. Finally, I could continue with Arthur's lesson.

But the spell had been broken and Arthur's usually jovial face looked unhappy, his mind seeming to be elsewhere.

"Arthur, your concentration is not very good today, so we shall finish now and have an extra half hour tomorrow. If the day is fine, we shall take a walk and discuss the Ten Commandments, perhaps going on to visit your family so that you can tell them what you have been learning."

"Thank you. I would like that" and, gathering his writing notes, he left quickly, without a backward glance. Really, both Hannah and Lucy were becoming too much of a nuisance. I would go to see Hannah immediately.

Chapter 53

Pushing open the bedchamber door, I strode in purposefully, not realising until now just how annoyed I felt that my precious time with dear Arthur was being spoiled by this girl. Without looking at Hannah, I spoke to Lucy,

"Lucy, leave me alone with Hannah. Go and help cook or speak to the housekeeper about what you can do to help her. It doesn't matter what you do or where you go, just leave."

"Yes, Mistress Margory, I shall go now – but she hasn't said a word since this morning."

"I'm here to deal with her now, Lucy. Just go."

With a backward glance at Hannah, she hurried off. It was only then that I turned to the girl.

"Hannah. In spite of all my generosity and time spent with you, I have yet again been interrupted in the duties which father has set for me. Hannah, open your eyes this very minute or I really shall become angry."

I sat on the edge of the bed. Hannah didn't move. I looked closer at the small face and suddenly felt my annoyance drain away. How pale she was. Beads of perspiration had collected on her forehead and I noticed that her chemise was wet. At that moment, her eyelashes flickered and her eyes opened a little.

"Mother. Is that you?"

What could she mean? My softening feelings began to be mixed with bewilderment.

"Of course I'm not your mother, Hannah. As you well know, she passed from this world several years ago."

She frowned.

"Then who are you? I want my mother. I wish to tell her that I have sinned."

What could be ailing the girl? And what did she mean? In what way had she sinned? Perhaps she had fallen asleep and was still dreaming.

"I shall ask Lucy to join you again, Hannah."

"Lucy?" She sneezed.

Clearly, she had no recollection of Lucy either. How strangely she was behaving. I would speak to mother. However, I wouldn't be able to do that until this evening or tomorrow, when we were breaking our fast, as she was attending a birth. She had said it might be a difficult delivery and on no account was she to be disturbed as the poor mother had had a painful time of late.

I was at a loss to understand what was happening to Hannah. It must be a cold. She had sneezed more than once when I was speaking to her. Yes, that's what it was – she was getting a cold. I felt a little relieved and comforted by this thought of her ailment being only a mild one.

Going to the kitchen, I found Lucy,

"You can go back to Hannah now, Lucy. But don't go too near as I think she's developing a cold."

A cold. Yes, that's what it must be. I went back to the library. If only mother was here. She would know what to do.

Not only was mother not at dinner, she was not able to join us at all for several days. Finally, I sent for the housekeeper, Goodwife Sykes, to ask for news.

"I've heard tell that it's a breech, Mistress Margory, and that neither the mother nor child may survive. It's very sad, and her Ladyship must be extremely tired."

"Goodwife Sykes. Usually, I would speak to mother about this, but I would like to ask your opinion."

"I'll help if I can, Mistress Margory."

"A few days ago, Lucy interrupted my teaching by telling me that Hannah was behaving strangely. I stopped teaching and went to see her, but she was sleeping. She appeared to be hot and was rambling, or perhaps coming out of a dream. Has Lucy said anything more to you? I'd hoped to speak to mother about it but, of course, haven't been able to. Has Lucy spoken to you about how Hannah is now?"

"I thought you knew, Mistress, although I have only just been told myself. Lucy has run off and hasn't been seen. I would normally have told your mother but she hasn't been here, and you are so busy now teaching that we didn't want to disturb you yet again."

Trying not to appear too perturbed, I said

"Would you go to see Hannah right away, Goodwife Sykes, and tell me what you think."

"I shall do that now, Mistress."

Chapter 54

I had never heard a scream like it, before or since, and I've heard plenty since. Rushing out of the library, I nearly ran into mother whose dark, circled eyes looked at me for a moment before whispering,

"What's going on, Margory? Can I not tend to the needs of our tenants without returning to Goodwife Sykes's screams that must have been heard throughout the county? I have been delayed, not only by an extremely difficult birth but, as the parson couldn't be found, I had to linger awhile to baptise the poor child, too."

Just then, the housekeeper appeared at the top of the great staircase, red in the face, her alarmed eyes large.

"Oh, my Lady, I'm so pleased to see you return, although I can see that you are very tired. It's Hannah, my Lady. She's as pale as death, not responding when I speak to her and not moving either."

"What? What happened to Lucy watching her and being there to ensure she was well?"

"Goodwife Sykes has only just told me, mother, that Lucy has run off and hasn't been seen."

"Get a bowl of water so we can see whether she is breathing. And hurry."

As the housekeeper rushed to the kitchen, I helped mother up the stairs to the room I had particularly chosen for Hannah. As we opened the door, a faint, fetid smell floated into our nostrils and mother groaned.

"How can this have happened in a few short days,

Margory? I thought Lucy was making sure that Hannah had all she needed and that you were visiting her regularly."

"I have visited her as often as I could, mother, and, when I saw her..."

I was interrupted by the housekeeper rushing in with a bowl of water which mother proceeded to place on Hannah's chest. If the water moved, she was breathing. It didn't.

"Goodwife Sykes. Go immediately and speak to Thomas, the Chief Groom. Tell him that he must take the fastest horse in the stables to summon our surgeon who must come as a matter of urgency. Tell him to tell the surgeon that it appears his patient is not breathing. Until he arrives, I must rest."

I didn't understand it. Hannah had a broken leg, so what had caused her apparent demise? There had been quite a lot of blood, too, I recalled, but I knew the surgeon had seen that, too. No, this was all Lucy's fault. It wasn't very long since I had visited Hannah – was it? It was Lucy who was her companion, ensuring she had someone to speak to and to inform us if Hannah deteriorated in any way. We must find Lucy and see what she had to say for herself. She must be hiding somewhere.

Arriving an hour later, the surgeon confirmed our fears with another bowl of water on Hannah's chest. She was indeed, not breathing and, he thought, she had been dead for, perhaps, two days. At mother's behest, he arranged for transport of the body to church.

Chapter 55

Mother said she felt a little rested but must tell the housekeeper to gather all the servants together. They looked at her expectantly.

"I have very sad news indeed, this day, I'm sorry to say. My daughter's maid, Hannah, has died. That is in spite of our getting the best of care for her by summoning our own, family surgeon. We also asked Lucy to stay with her so that she had a companion at all times of day and night. And to ensure that she was amused, my dear daughter herself visited Hannah regularly to read to her.

It now appears that Lucy has run off. Did she speak to anyone before she went? Does anyone know where she is? I do know that, like Hannah, she has no relatives in Hertfordshire, and, it may be that she has no relatives anywhere. So I am concerned for her safety."

One of the servants spoke up,

"Your Ladyship, I heard one of the grooms saying he thought he'd seen someone who looked like Lucy out on the main highway. When he asked her if she was all right, she said she was waiting for someone, she wouldn't say who. He said he wasn't absolutely sure it was her as he hadn't seen her very often."

"That is grave news indeed, as a young woman on her own on these roads is in great danger. What could have made her take such a risk?"

"Your Ladyship. What did Hannah die of?"

The abrupt interruption and change of subject made everyone turn to stare at Arthur. I, myself, wondered about his interest. Perhaps I should add kindness to his list of good qualities.

"That is, indeed, a good question, Arthur, the answer to which even the surgeon is not sure. He thinks it possible she may have contracted a fever, with a high temperature and, with no means of lowering her temperature, her mind may have been affected."

"Begging your pardon, your Ladyship, but why do you say that there was no means of lowering her temperature? Although it seems that Lucy ran away, leaving Hannah alone, Mistress Margory said that she was visiting her regularly. Was this fever and high temperature not apparent to Mistress Margory?"

A few of the servants gasped, as his implication was clear. It was then I thought I heard it whispered,

"I think she died of sadness and loneliness."

Then, so softly, that I thought I may have misheard,

"Nonsense, she died of neglect. The mistress has been otherwise occupied."

"What, with the ball arrangements, do you mean?"

"No, that isn't what I mean."

I looked around, trying to see who was saying such things, but everyone then stopped speaking. My mind was racing, and I asked myself again. Why was Arthur asking such a question so boldly? Perhaps it wasn't kindness at all, but because he had cared for Hannah?

Softly and calmly, mother answered him,

"Your concern for your fellow servant is very touching, Arthur, particularly as I understand that you and Hannah were becoming friends. However, I am sure you realise that kindness is also one of my dear daughter's traits. Instead of putting Hannah into one of the servants' bedchambers, on the lower floor of The Manor, when she slipped and broke her leg, it was Mistress Margory's suggestion to couch her in one of our own, beautiful bedchambers on the upper floor. Also, it was her decision to tell Lucy to stay with Hannah at all times. Not only did Lucy not do that, but she clearly left Hannah at a time when she was needed most. I must also point out to you, Arthur, that it was his Lordship's decision to take up your education by having reading, writing and arithmetic taught to you. You are fortunate indeed that these subjects are being taught because of the charitable nature of my own daughter. I am sure you realise that this is very unusual and it is something that I, myself, questioned as I wasn't sure whether it was either wise or necessary. However, not once did Mistress Margory question the appropriateness of teaching you herself. Because of that commitment, she was not able to visit Hannah as often as she would have liked, I am sure. Also, as you know, the whole household is preparing for a ball, to be held in a week's time, which means that everyone is particularly busy at the moment."

Arthur's bold question was surprising. However, at that moment my attention was diverted as I became aware of sniggers and giggles from a few of the servants when mother had pointed out my thoughtfulness in the teaching of Arthur.

Mother continued,

"Go back to your duties, all of you. His Lordship

will be returning later and I must take to my bed for a short time. The delivery that has been the cause of my absence for the last few days was an extremely difficult one. The mother and child are no longer with us and I am very tired as well as extremely sad. This is the first time I have had such a result and I need time to recover somewhat."

Indeed, mother could barely climb the stairs, so I quickly ran to her aid. I could see how upset she was and how these deaths had affected her deeply. When I offered my help, she said,

"Thank you, Margory, but it would be more helpful to me if you could now take over the household for the next few hours until I am feeling sufficiently rested to join you and father for dinner. I doubt that cook, good cook that she is, has given a thought to our meals for the rest of the week. Please go and speak to her, as well as to the housekeeper, to ensure that the house begins to run as smoothly as it does when I am here all the time."

I had never seen mother looking so exhausted, so I readily agreed to do as she asked. I would have to cancel Arthur's lessons for the moment. I would give him some work to do, and tell him that I would see him and the completed work the week following the ball. It would do him good to be out of my company for a little while. Particularly after his earlier outspokenness.

Chapter 56

When I went to the library, Arthur was already standing at the door.

"In view of Lady Francis's words, I don't want you to think that I'm ungrateful for the lessons you're giving me, Mistress Margory. I'm really enjoying them. My parents are proud that his Lordship has not only invited me to dine with your family, but that I am also learning about words and numbers."

"Yes, yes, Arthur. I haven't got time to spend chattering to you now. I must organise the household until my mother feels rested. Also, I am very much looking forward to the ball next week and to renewing my acquaintanceship with the gentlemen I have met here, in Hertfordshire, at The Manor and in London as well as at the home of my aunt in Gloucester. Their conversation is most interesting because, of course, they are educated young men with whom I am able to have interesting conversations about art and music. I am, indeed, looking forward to seeing them again. I am too busy to do it now, but tomorrow morning I shall prepare work for you to do in reading and writing for the next week. Come to me at 3 of the clock sharp and I shall show you what to do. Our classes will resume the week after the ball."

Although Arthur's look of disappointment made me feel weak at the knees, I looked away momentarily so that my feelings were not echoed in the look I then gave him. It was a look he wasn't used to receiving from me. He had to be taught a lesson, a lesson that did not involve reading, writing or arithmetic.

"Also, Arthur, I think that until the ball is over, it might be more appropriate for you to resume your place with the servants for the main meals of the day. Mother is very tired and there will be personal, family discussions about Hannah, Lucy and the ball which will be uninteresting for an outsider, such as a servant, like yourself. Mother has placed responsibility for organisation of the household into my hands for the moment, so I shall tell her and father that the three of us will be dining alone until after the ball."

This was an unexpected turn of events for Arthur whose shoulders sagged at my words. I knew how much he enjoyed the privilege of being seated with my family at the dining table. Also, as he shared my own love of learning, he was doing very well at writing and reading. Although I had not told him so, I would soon be starting to teach him his favourite subject of arithmetic. But perhaps mother had been right in saying that he should not be included in our lives as much as he had been for the past two weeks. His outburst and improper questioning of mother regarding Hannah's death, as well as the question he had raised regarding my care of her indicated that he still had the mind of a servant. The indulgent treatment he had received from my generous father must stop for the moment, and I must harden my heart whenever I saw his handsome, laughing face. It would do him good to be denied the company of me and my family. However, I could not ignore a question that rose up and tapped me on the shoulder. How could I consider being without his company, day after day, for a whole ten days? My heart answered very clearly. I could not bear the thought. But he must be taught a lesson.

Chapter 57

I told mother that I felt too ill and sad to go to Hannah's funeral. It wasn't necessary, after all, as my parents had arranged more than usual for our impecunious servant; she was even going to be buried in the churchyard, where, mother said, a small, remote corner had been found after my generous father had made it worth the Parson's while. Mother responded,

"Well, in that case you must rest, my dear, because the ball is being given in your honour, and you must be feeling refreshed and well."

It was not possible, of course, for me to avoid the ball. Once again, cook had prepared some sumptuous dishes and once again, the gown I wore was extremely pretty and suited my newly curvaceous, although slender body very well. I wore my new silk indigo gown with its silver thread. It had a particularly closely fitted bodice and, although that made breathing difficult, it was worth it. The young Gentlemen whom I had described to Arthur were, indeed, well travelled and well educated so I did enjoy talking to them about France and Italy as well as the artists they had met whose work they had bought. They, in turn, admired my dress, but soon passed on to talk to other, prettier young women. But now, I cared not. My heart was becoming closer to a young man who was just as handsome, if not more so, than they were.

When I saw mother she said,

"Well, my dear, I'm delighted to see you paying interest in these very eligible young men. They are all heirs to magnificent houses, and your father and I would be delighted to see you joined to any of them. Remember that they are of our social status and have enjoyed a similar upbringing to your own. We would be proud to see you take their name and have a family who are brought up in the way you are used to."

I nodded dutifully, but my eyes and thoughts were rarely away from Arthur. He had been told to help with the serving of champagne and canapés; I had added that, when I used my whistle, he was to serve me immediately. Although a shocked look had crossed his face for a moment, I ignored it; he needed to realise the superiority of my family and friends. However, although I knew that my attitude would please mother, I didn't feel entirely comfortable and resorted to only using the whistle once, and only then, softly. Also, when I saw his wonderful face, I turned to one of the Gentlemen in the group in an animated fashion, appearing to be giving all my attention to him and to be enjoying his company very much. When I slid the occasional glance at Arthur, I was happy to see that he had noticed and that he seemed rather downcast. That was the only part of the ball that made me happy. After all, it was important that Arthur cared for me as much as I for him. Also, try as I might – and, really, I was not trying very hard – none of these young men interested me at all and neither were they interested in me. It would take more than a ball for me to become the mistress of one of their fine houses. Besides, my heart now lay elsewhere.

Eventually, the interminably long day came to an end and I fixed a smile on my face as I bade the guests goodbye. I would retire early so that I could ride Chestnut in the morning and prepare myself for my afternoon session with Arthur. Although I felt very sorry that Hannah had become ill and died, I had spent several hours a week with her, time that I really did not have to spare and that I would now have to devote particularly to teaching Arthur. I must also speak to mother about who would become my new personal maid. I had noticed an older servant called Ruth. She seemed to be very capable, quiet and humble, and I thought that she would do very well. I would suggest that she be given a month's trial to see how well she coped with the daughter of the mistress of the house. Above all, she must be discreet. I hadn't yet forgotten the whispering and giggles that had accompanied Arthur's outburst. Also, my absence at Hannah's funeral had not gone unnoticed. I would round a corner in the house to find a gaggle of chattering servants, whose conversations ceased the moment they saw me. All that must stop, although I knew that tittle-tattle was almost impossible to prevent. I would need to be more careful in future in my dealings with Arthur. However high my heart leapt at the sight of him, I must remain dignified. I was, after all, the daughter of the Lord of The Manor.

Chapter 58

Arthur's knock on the library door was prompt that day. Good. His manners were improving. He was learning that, when one makes an appointment, particularly when that appointment is with Gentry, that one should not be late; it is inconsiderate and would not be tolerated. I nevertheless paused for a moment before allowing his entrance. Just sufficient time for my blushing to subside and my beating heart to slow. Arthur seemed to be very quick to notice such things. Once calm, I called him in.

"Enter. Oh, it's you, Arthur. Is that the time already? I've been enjoying myself so much today that your lesson had completely eluded me. Do come in and take a seat. I'm looking forward to seeing the work you've done and, if it's as good as I hope, we may soon be embarking on arithmetic. Would you like that?"

"I would like that very much, Mistress Margory. Thank you."

"Good. Then let's begin by my looking through the work you've done for me to see how well you've progressed. I've felt very unhappy for quite some time now because of Hannah's accident and death, but we must put all that behind us. Nothing can bring her back, however much we would like that to happen. However, before we begin, I need to talk to you about a concern of mine.

I've heard some of the servants chattering about the lessons you're having with me. One of the things you need to learn, Arthur, now that you are fortunate enough to be taking meals and conversing with my parents and me is that our conversations must not be repeated to any of the other servants. Nor should idle conversation regarding myself or either of my parents be allowed to go unaddressed. Should you hear any of the servants speaking about any of us, you must exercise discretion. Discretion is a word I would like you to learn today. Its meaning includes not revealing private conversations, nor causing offence by speaking out of turn. Am I making myself clear, Arthur?"

"Perfectly, Mistress Margory."

But I didn't really hear his reply because I was looking into those big, blue eyes which were looking at me in such a way that, had I not been seated already, my knees would have turned to wool.

Chapter 59

I did feel, now, that my life was becoming increasingly happy. Arthur once again joined mother, father and I for our main meals and he continued with his classes with me five days a week. At the end of one of them, I told him,

"Now that you're becoming proficient in reading and writing and will soon be starting arithmetic, Arthur, I think it's time to speak to father about your joining in the hawking and hunting. Would you like that?

"Most certainly, Mistress Margory. However, my horse is getting old and it wouldn't be appropriate to ride alongside the fine horses of the Gentry."

"I quite agree, Arthur. I shall speak to father to see if anything can be done. We have many horses so I shall ask him whether you can ride one of those. Of course, the horse would be a loan only, it would not be a gift."

"Of course not, and thank you very much indeed. You're very good to me, Mistress Margory."

My heart leapt a little at his compliment, but I was determined not to show that to Arthur.

"Nonsense! I treat all the servants equally. It's father to whom you owe thanks. He chose you as his manservant and you have proven to be worthy of the trust he has in you and the responsibilities he has given you."

Arthur then spoke unexpectedly,

"May I speak to you about a personal matter, Mistress?"

"Of course, anything."

My palms felt a little damp at this turn in the conversation. Was he about to declare his love for me? If so, how would I receive such a declaration? But, disappointingly, my wondering was unnecessary.

"Some of the other servants are saying that I am being given special privileges that I have not earned. I've now been fortunate enough to join your family at the meal table for some time. Also, my reading, writing and soon to be arithmetical knowledge is setting me apart in a way that makes them jealous and spiteful. Those who are my friends know that these opportunities were offered to me by your father, while others think that there is another reason. When his lordship suggested these classes, I thought that the other servants would be happy for me. However, I've learned that some are and some are not, and I'm not sure how to deal with this. I would welcome your advice, Mistress Margory."

"I am, indeed, glad that you have told me about this, Arthur, as I have begun to notice it, too. We must remember that this is just idle chatter. While, often, there is no malice in such tongue-wagging, sometimes it can be harmful. I shall think about what you have said in case I decide that something must be done. However, in the meantime, please remember what I have told you. If you should hear any conversations that are damaging to father, mother or myself, then please tell me who has said what."

But Arthur continued. He was clearly uneasy and I, myself, abhorred such idle chatter, so could understand his anxiety.

"I am, of course, happy to speak to the people concerned myself, Mistress, most of whom I care not for anyway. However, there are a few servants who I would not want to be misled into thinking that you are teaching me for reasons other than reading, writing and arithmetic. On a few occasions I've asked the cause of their laughter so that I may join them but they've said that I may not find it amusing."

I was pleased to hear that Arthur was challenging these conversations, but irritated that the servants were, perhaps, finding me the source of merriment – for I was fairly sure I was the reason for their cackling. It raised a dilemma for me. Under normal circumstances, I would have gone straight to mother for her sensible advice. However, on this occasion, I felt that advising mother about the possible reason for the servants' chattering may make her more determined than ever to curtail my association with Arthur. She may even suggest to father that it was not good for Arthur to be separated from those of his own class by joining us at meal times. That, I could not risk. No, this was a matter for father. He and I had planned to go riding that very day, so I would use that opportunity to speak to him then.

Chapter 60

It was a beautiful, late autumnal day. The leaves were bronze, ochre and vivid red and next year's harvest had just been sown. The air was warm and all was peace and tranquillity; the only sound was that of the birds swooping around us and the canter of the horses' hooves. Father and I rode in companionable silence. His time was so taken with local political affairs and the undulating religious fervour, that he barely had time to rest. A ride out together was a delightful and rare occurrence. I knew I must try not to spoil it by raising a trivial matter, particularly as that would usually be something my mother dealt with. But I needn't have worried, for father raised a subject himself which gave me a natural entree to my concern.

"Arthur is obviously thoroughly enjoying his classes with you and, from what he says, he is learning very fast. It will not be long now until Stephen retires from my service and takes up occupancy of one of the cottages on our land. I'm very pleased to see Arthur growing in confidence and knowledge of my needs. He seems to know what I want before I have even asked, which is extremely helpful and saves me precious time. He also obviously has a flair for arithmetic and wants to try his hand at some of my everyday accounts. This will also free some time for me to pursue more important matters. Yes, I couldn't be more pleased with his progress."

"It's on the subject of Arthur that I would like to ask your advice, father. It's only a trivial matter, and I'm sorry about that, as normally I would speak to mother. However, I don't wish to trouble her further at the moment. I think she's still feeling rather tired and upset about the death of the mother and child."

"You're quite right, my dear. She feels their loss deeply. It is made even worse by the fact that she rarely loses either mother or babe. So to lose both... Well, her sadness is difficult for me to see.

But what is this subject you would like my advice about, my dear? Matters regarding the servants are, as you say, usually for your mother to resolve, as I have neither the time nor the inclination to be involved. There is a great deal of what we landowners are calling land grabbing happening at the moment, for example, which is occupying more of my time than I would wish. However, if this is something that would cause your mother concern, I certainly don't wish to burden her further."

"This is my worry, father. Arthur has told me that he thinks he and I may be the subject of idle chatter in our household, although he can't be sure because their whisperings stop the moment he is seen. I'm concerned that this may spread outside our household to the other great houses in Hertfordshire and I wonder what can be done to make sure it doesn't happen."

"The short answer, my dear, is that nothing can be done. Unkind conversations will always spread, due to their seemingly exciting nature. Neither you, mother or I can stop them. However, I am, indeed, pleased that you have brought this to my attention. It may be, in fact, that something can be done to stem its rise. What we can try to do is to keep the household informed when a change occurs, either by your mother, yourself or, even, occasionally, by me. I have often found that, when people are told the true facts, there is little left to chatter about. As I have already said, Stephen will be retiring from my service very soon and Arthur will be taking his place. In the light of what you have just told me, I shall tell mother to gather the entire household together in order to make that announcement myself. That should stop any further incorrect conversations. However, my dear, you should realise, it will not stop them all."

* * *

Dear Diary,

Dear, dear father. How very wise he is. I knew he'd have the answer. He always does. Today, he did exactly as he said he would. Mother told the housekeeper to gather the household together for the important announcement. My father is well respected by everyone and, while there was obvious surprise on some faces, most of the servants knew that Arthur would be taking over from Stephen at some time. So I intend to put this foolishness behind me. I'm now a step closer to Arthur being mine. He's a fine young man who is becoming as good a Gentleman as can be found anywhere in the county. I have also noticed how some of the young ladies of the great houses look appreciatively at him. Any one of them would be happy to be seen on his arm, but no one else will take that familiar position. That arm belongs to me and me alone.

Chapter 61

Now that Arthur was father's chief manservant, he was able to buy clothes that befitted his station, when out of uniform. I noticed that now, for our daily classes, he changed out of that uniform and into a particularly smart jerkin over his doublet. I knew that this provoked more chatter, but I ignored it. Twice a week, we were also riding and I had temporarily given him a stallion from my own stables until he was able to buy his own. How fine he looked astride the horse and what a good horseman he was! Even mother was beginning to change her view of him, although slowly.

At meal one day I was surprised when he addressed my parents directly; he usually remained fairly quiet at meal times, partly, I think, because he was concentrating on ensuring his table manners were as they should be. If he looked unsure, I always quietly helped him and, deep in conversation as my parents were, increasingly, these days, I think they hardly noticed.

"If it pleases you, sir, may I be so bold as to ask your permission to carry out an activity which has been long on my mind?"

My parents stopped what they were doing and, looking at Arthur, they both nodded.

"Of course, Arthur. What is it? I hope that you are well and enjoying your new duties. I certainly continue to be happy with your work."

"Oh yes, Sir, I'm very well, and am delighted to be of greater service to you. What I wished to say was that in one month's time it's my parents' 25th wedding anniversary and they are planning a hog roast. All the tenants are invited and I would be honoured to take Mistress Margory as my very special guest. But only with your permission, of course."

The surprise and delight on my face was obvious to both my parents, who had turned to look at me. I was very pleased that it was mother who replied.

"Certainly, Arthur, you have our permission, provided Mistress Margory herself agrees, of course. She knows all our tenants very well, having seen some of them since birth, so I am happy for you to ask her yourself."

My face said it all and my reply was superfluous, really.

"I should be delighted, Arthur, to accompany you to your parents' feast; I'll enter it into my diary this very day."

Then, turning to mother, I said,

"Would you help me to choose a gift for Arthur's parents, mother. Twenty-five years of marriage is a wonderful achievement and one I would like to mark by giving them something special."

Waving aside Arthur's objection, I smiled at him so lovingly that I thought my feelings must be obvious to everyone. Blushing, I dropped my head and started to fold my napkin.

"I have an even better idea!" Father looked quite animated.

"I must go to London in the middle of next week to meet my friend, William Garrard, who has done a considerable amount of very valuable work with the poor, of whom, it grieves me to say, there are many thousands in London. But that is the only meeting I have arranged on this occasion. I shall reserve rooms at my usual, excellent inn, The White Hart on Drury Lane; Margory and Arthur will accompany my wife and me. We shall stay for two nights. Arthur will accompany me to my meeting on the first day and we shall all enjoy a fine dinner each evening. That will give Margory and her mother an opportunity to shop to their hearts' content. Oh, I know how much you ladies enjoy the shops. While there, my wife will help Margory to choose something appropriate and special for your parents, Arthur. How does that sound?"

It was one of the best notions I had heard in a very long time and I gazed my delighted approbation at my father.

Arthur was also clearly very pleased.

"Why Sir, I thank you very much indeed. It will certainly be an honour to accompany you and your family on such a trip. I shall start to prepare for your important meeting immediately. I shall also speak to Thomas to ensure that horses are ready for the journey."

"Thank you, Arthur. I'm pleased to see that you are removing some of these sorts of duties from me which is very helpful. While the horse you have been using from my daughter's stable is suitable for your riding on my land, it will be more appropriate for you to take Sapphire, a stallion, from my own stables for our journey to London."

Knowing how much Arthur enjoyed riding, I was

delighted that father had made this offer to him. Since Arthur had started to play a large part in my life, I had become increasingly content. And now that my family was including him in this special journey, my happiness was quite overwhelming. I turned to my mother,

"Dear mother. Is there anything I can do to help you today? It has been a little while since I helped you with a birthing and, although I have now witnessed many, I would like to help with another."

"I'm very pleased that you have mentioned that, Margory as I do miss the help that Lucy used to give me, in your absence. I think, in fact, the time has come for you to manage a birthing yourself and, on the first few occasions, I shall accompany you to ensure that all is well. However, I have great confidence in your abilities. It is clear that you are very fond of babies as well as children in general. You have a natural ability in midwifery which I am very pleased to see. You also have a very tender and kind way of dealing with the mothers which helps them greatly to endure their pain with fortitude. Yes, I don't think it will be very long before we can consider your becoming licensed. I shall be happy, my dear, to ask your father to pay the £2 fee."

This was, indeed, high praise from my mother. Her reputation of having excellent midwifery skills was well known, not only to our tenants, but to the other great houses in the county, who were known to ask her advice.

Chapter 62

Arthur's classes and my own preparations for this very special journey to London flew by on a cloud of the utmost pleasure. Nothing could go wrong and no one would stand in the way of making Arthur mine now. Even when I turned a corner in The Manor and encountered mutterings behind hands, my mood was not to be darkened. When I looked back, the journey to London was the beginning of the happiest time in my life – or so I thought – and I wondered whether such utter bliss could continue indefinitely. It was to prove not.

With father and Arthur riding in front, flanked by two of our grooms, mother and I rode close behind with four other grooms and our maids, Ruth and Beatrice. Thieves were known to be everywhere and were particularly drawn to groups such as ours who appeared to be wealthy, of course. Father always made a point of carrying very little money and stayed in only the best inns in London, where he was well known and at which the staff did not collude with highwaymen. His responsibility, and that of his grooms, was even greater when any of his family travelled with him. He had insisted that my mother and I did not wear costly riding outfits, nor that we included valuable jewellery in our cases. We had heard horrific stories of friends who had been attacked, robbed and left for dead. Indeed, one of father's business colleagues had been killed, and, since then, father had taken additional grooms on his journeys to London. But I felt perfectly safe, not only because mother and I were under father's protection but because

I knew that Arthur – just like the legendary King – was very brave and would not allow any harm to befall us. He would regularly cast a glance over his shoulder at mother and me and I responded with the happiest of smiles. He could not, however, do anything about the dreadful sights at most of the crossroads leading into London. On this occasion, the gallows were particularly gruesome, with dismembered, rotting bodies, their entrails being picked at by scavenging birds, their eyes gone by the same, constant pecking. I didn't look closer as I'd heard stories of men's private parts that were so dreadful that surely they couldn't be believed. The breeze, although slight, was effective in carrying the most abominable, putrid smell, forcing us to draw our capes across our nostrils. When the most hideous of these sights loomed into sight, Arthur turned his horse and joined mother and me. He told me to change horses and ride behind him so that I could bury my face in his broad back. That was so enjoyable, I almost forgot about the dreadful bodies.

But suddenly, without warning, a group of knife- and pistol-wielding, masked men galloped at speed out of the woods. They rode towards father and the two grooms. They must have been following us and, on seeing Arthur leave father, had taken the opportunity to rob us.

Arthur immediately took charge, shouting to the four grooms,

"Defend his Lordship!"

With me clinging on to him, Arthur then wheeled his horse around to my mother's. She was screaming so much I thought she would faint. I closed my eyes and prayed that Arthur and father would beat off these brutal men. We watched as father drew out his purse, containing only a few coins, and threw it at them,

"That is all I have and you're welcome to it."

Sensing they had chosen someone from whom they would gain little, the men turned their attention to us, shouting,

"We'll see whether that's all the money you carry when we have your comely ladies at our mercy."

I swear that mother's shouts could be heard in the middle of London itself. The rest happened so quickly I wasn't really sure who had done what to whom. All I could hear was mother screaming even louder, and, just as the grooms were reaching for their pistols, everything went quiet. A single loud crack had sounded, and the leader of the group fell. While we all gazed at Arthur's smoking weapon, the gang scooped up their leader and rode off, without a backward glance.

We were all stunned for a moment. Silence enclosed us. Until mother whispered, sobbing,

"I cannot go on, I must turn back and return home."

Her face was pale, her eyes large and she was trembling from head to foot. Father went to her side, lifted her down from her horse and walked away a few paces, speaking softly to her.

"It isn't much further now to the inn, dearest, where you will be able to have a long, hot bath and change into one of your pretty dresses. I shall not allow you to return home, even though some of the grooms would accompany you. It would be much too dangerous.

Collect yourself, my dear. The thieves have gone and, thanks to Arthur, we are all safe, just a little shaken."

"I am more than a little shaken, husband, and shall not be taking this journey again. As though the sight of the gallows is not enough, to be attacked by rogues is more than I can bear. You must not ask me to risk my life again."

"I understand, my dear. For the remainder of the journey, I shall tell Arthur to ride with you and Margory. He has proven himself well able to protect us and, although I am sorry to see that someone has lost their life, who knows whether any of us would have lived, had Arthur not taken the action he did."

Still trembling from head to foot, mother walked to where Arthur had dismounted. He was steadying his horse while speaking to me, making sure that I was all right.

"My dear boy. How can I thank you enough? The speed with which you drew your pistol and despatched that dreadful threat was really quite remarkable. I had no idea you had such skills, nor that you were even carrying a pistol."

In speaking to Arthur, mother was gradually regaining her dignity and composure. She still was unsure whether to treat him as yet another servant. However, she was now beginning to realise that, in opposing his rise in the household, she was increasingly taking a lone stance.

Knowing how difficult it was for mother to speak to him in this way, Arthur, my chivalrous Arthur, addressed her gently,

"Your Ladyship. I am so very sorry to have seen you upset in this way by rogues of the road. Any Lady such as yourself would have reacted in exactly the way that you did, given your sweet-tempered disposition. I immediately knew that I could not allow even one hair of your handsome head to be touched. My thought was to immediately ensure the safety of your good self and Mistress Margory. When you are distressed, I am also distressed. I merely did what any man would have done, given the circumstances of this outrage. I am indeed very glad that you are safe and unharmed. Under the circumstances, I thought you were very courageous."

Throughout this pretty speech, I could see that mother was feeling a surprise she was trying to suppress.

"I can see that you are not only becoming a learned young man but that you are also exceedingly charming and brave. And for that, I thank you."

With that, and beginning to regain a little of her imperious demeanour, she returned to her horse, where the groom assisted in her re-mounting. She was then heard to urge father on.

"Let us continue, husband. Hurry, if you will. Do not delay us. This evening, we shall all enjoy a hearty meal, at which we shall toast Arthur with the best wine the cellar has to offer."

Father and I exchanged glances, father's showing that he would clearly never understand the workings of the female mind. My lightening heart engaged my mouth in a small smile. I understood what was happening here and I was glad of it.

The remainder of the journey passed without incident, other than the occasional naked men on the gallows. I was even becoming used to seeing those. As they loomed in the distance, Arthur indicated their imminent location and I turned away my head. When we finally arrived at The White Hart Inn, mother and father were exhausted. However, Arthur and I were enjoying renewed energy as a result of his having gained elevated status, particularly in the eyes of mother. In my eyes, of course, Arthur could rarely do any wrong.

When my maid, Ruth, had prepared my bath, unpacked my dresses and put out my green silk, she waited.

"Did you not think, Ruth, that Master Arthur was extremely brave today? My father, of course, is also brave, but a little older, so his reactions are not quite so swift. The thieves were very frightening and I dare not imagine what would have happened to mother and me had Master Arthur not taken charge in the way he did. He showed them that we were not to be trifled with. Were you not frightened, too, Ruth?"

"Yes, Mistress Margory, I thought we would all be killed. But Master Arthur was totally without fear. I thanked the Lord when he did what he did."

"When you have helped me to dress, Ruth, you are free to go to your room and spend the evening as you wish. I shall not require your help until tomorrow morning."

"Yes, Mistress. I hope you have a good evening with your parents and Master Arthur. Am I to assume that Master Arthur will be dining with you this evening?"

"What a foolish question, Ruth, of course he will. Master Arthur is proving to be extremely helpful to father, particularly as he can now read, write and do arithmetic increasingly well. Father has a meeting tomorrow to which he will take Master Arthur while you and I, mother and Beatrice will enjoy the shops. In fact, I am feeling particularly generous at the moment, so that if you see a manicure set that you like, I shall buy it for you. But, of course, I must mainly look for a wedding anniversary present for Master Arthur's parents."

Ruth's face brightened. I knew that she was harbouring affection for one of the young manservants, which was partly why I had chosen her to succeed Hannah. I didn't intend to risk the introduction of another pretty young maid into my personal everyday life. No, Ruth would discover that I was a very good employer, provided she behaved in a way that pleased me.

Chapter 63

What a feast met our eyes as we entered our private room at the inn! The table groaned beneath the weight of trenchers bearing haunch of venison, sea bream, woodpigeon and suckling pig. The smell was divine and I could barely restrain myself from starting to eat immediately, lifting the meats with my fingers until the juices and sauces were running down my hand and arm. I put the daily washed napery to good use and cared not at all for the spotlessly clean table linen. Sitting by my side, Arthur was watching me carefully as I sipped a little wine, while his glass was never empty.

The gown I'd chosen to wear was perhaps not what mother would have thought to be appropriate, but I was feeling so happy I cared not. It was one that I had bought in London when accompanying father on the last visit, so it was the latest fashion. Mother had not yet seen it, so her swift, appraising look was not lost on me. The skirt was very full, the waist small, the neck sufficiently low to reveal a little, but not so low as to be improper. I had brought a second gown that mother would most certainly not regard as being proper but, again, I felt so happy, I would take that risk. After all, once married, I, myself, would not deem it appropriate to wear such necklines.

When the meats and fish had been devoured, the trenchers were cleared and the sweetmeats were brought in, all the while our wine glasses being filled. The innkeeper knew my father was a very good guest who lodged with him regularly. He intended this to be a very special occasion. Oranges, figs and pomegranates were piled high, together with cherries, marchpane, Dishes of Snow, Jumballs and honeyed plums. I could see that Arthur had never been so close to such culinary delights which encouraged me to press him to take his fill even more. Mother and father had been deep in conversation and I could see that mother was now becoming very tired and would not long be to bed. Moving a little closer to Arthur, I reached across his broad chest, taking my time in choosing a particularly succulent plum which appeared to be just a little beyond my reach. This brought me even closer to him and, dipping a little, I ensured that my breasts were revealed even more, something that was not lost on him, I was glad to see.

"I do beg your pardon, Arthur. That plum looked particularly delicious."

As I leaned back, I bit into the ripeness and allowed the juices to run down my chin and breasts, only delaying a moment in which I saw Arthur's eyes watching the juice. In that second, I longed for his tongue to follow the route of the juice and further.

"The plums do look exceedingly delicious. Perhaps I shall have more wine and try them myself later."

Mother suddenly seemed wide awake. I hadn't noticed that her conversation with father had stopped and all seemed very still while she took in this intimate scene. She cleared her throat before addressing me,

"I think it is time for us to retire, my dear, and leave the men to their port and business discussions. I believe we are delaying them."

Had I looked again at Arthur, I would not have been able to accede to mother's suggestion. However, I didn't intend to irritate her just when she was beginning to realise how much of a Gentleman he was becoming. Taking my time, I resumed my previous position further from Arthur. I then stood and, patting my gown into tidiness, allowed the tips of my fingers to trace the line of my bosom.

"Good night, father. Good night Arthur. I hope you both have very sweet dreams."

I felt sure that Arthur's dreams would be very sweet indeed.

With Ruth's help, I undressed, doused the candles, climbed into the very comfortable bed, with its large, soft pillows, and lay there thinking about the day of adventure and wonderful evening. I was learning more about Arthur every day. Today I had witnessed how very brave he was and how extremely charming he could be. When we had left home, mother had accepted Arthur's presence as a nuisance that she had to bear. By the end of the evening, he had risen in her eyes to such a degree that even I was surprised. As I drifted into a happy, contented sleep, I thought I heard a soft tapping at my door. It must have been the beginning of my beautiful dream.

Chapter 64

The following morning, father, Arthur and I sat quietly to break our fast, mother having told father that she was beginning to feel the after-effects of the previous day's shock; she hadn't slept very well and would join us a little later. After father and Arthur had left for the meeting, I went to mother's room and she did, indeed, look very tired and pale.

"Today, my dear, while I am happy to accompany you and help to choose Arthur's parents' gift, I am feeling exhausted and shall only be able to walk slowly. I can't wait to return to the country, away from these scavenging pigs and kites that lurk around every corner of this town. Let us take a small ale before leaving, then father has told me of a very good inn that serves tasty meals and where I may rest a while."

I felt so very contented that I was happy to agree to anything mother might suggest. Choosing a gift did not prove to be easy. It had to be something that the grooms could carry in their panniers as, to have it sent, would mean its arriving after the festivities. Also, I did not want to embarrass Arthur's parents by choosing something which was so expensive they would be afraid to put it into use. Finally, I settled on several pomanders that contained sweet smelling herbs and spices; they could be worn on the person or spread around the cottage to douse both the smell of smoke and other noxious scents.

We returned to the inn late in the afternoon and, after a glass of wine, mother and I examined my purchases, deciding that they had, indeed, been a good choice. They were not only sweet-smelling and very practical, they looked very pretty, too.

"I think that I shall retire to my room now, Margory. I am extremely tired and tomorrow we shall have to endure the ride back to The Manor. I am already feeling anxious in case we should be set upon again. Also, the thought of those dreadful bodies on the gallows... Well, it will be some time before I venture into London again. I am perfectly content to stay in Hertfordshire and to entertain at The Manor as well as visiting our neighbours. However, I now know that, should we be attacked, Arthur will do all he can to dismiss the rogues – as, of course, will father and the grooms."

"I suspect that word has travelled abroad, too, mother, that the leader of the thieves has been despatched, so that others may be reluctant to approach us."

"You are quite right, my dear. However, I shall, nevertheless, be much comforted when we enter our own estate once again. In the meantime, I shall rest and ask the innkeeper to send a light meal to my room."

"That sounds very wise, mother. Rest well so that you are prepared for the return journey tomorrow. Is there anything I can get for you before I bathe and change for the evening meal?"

"What a good daughter you are, Margory. No, I have everything I need. Please ask Beatrice to come to help me disrobe and bathe."

"Of course, mother. Sleep well." With that, I kissed

her affectionately.

Returning to my room, I looked at the two other gowns I had brought and decided on the crimson silk. It was more daring than I usually wore and I had not yet worn it. Nor was I sure that mother would approve, so this evening would be an ideal time to wear it, knowing that she wouldn't be troubled by my boldness. Showing Ruth my purchases for Arthur's parents, I asked her to perfume my bath, using the special, perfumed soap that I had brought with me. Recalling the previous, sad accident with Hannah, I also told her to be very careful when walking around the bath. On assuring me that she would, she commented,

"What a beautiful gown, Mistress, and so very fashionable."

When I stepped out of the bath and dried myself on the linen towel, Ruth helped me to put on the farthingale and linen chemise before the final gown itself. Although the ruff was beginning to be high fashion, I didn't personally care for it, but preferred the low cut, square neckline, corseted bodice and cinched in waist.

I waited until I knew that father and Arthur would be already seated before joining them. Pretending not to notice Arthur's look of surprise when I bent to kiss father on the cheek, I took a seat opposite Arthur. My father said,

"Well, my dear, although mother tells me that she will be resting in our room rather than joining us at dinner, she tells me that your visit to the shops was successful today."

"I'm happy to say that it was, father, and I do hope that Arthur's parents enjoy my gifts."

Arthur was quick to respond,

"Oh, I'm sure that, whatever they are, my parents will be delighted that you have spent time so generously in choosing something for their special occasion."

As before, the innkeeper had provided an excellent meal, although I noticed that Arthur seemed rather distracted whenever I reached for a delicacy, and he ate very little. Indeed, when I asked if he liked my new dress, I thought he might choke.

"It's...er...very pretty and very becoming."

In fact, his cheeks were becoming rather flushed, I noticed, but I simply smiled and thanked him.

Once again, that night, I thought I heard a knock on my chamber door, but I must have been dreaming. Dreams are strange things, aren't they? So I pulled the beautifully clean sheets over my head and slept peacefully.

Chapter 65

Mother was feeling very rested the following morning and, when we had broken our fast, the innkeeper wished us a warm farewell and we left. Father rode with the two groomsmen, mother and I with four, our maids and Arthur, who insisted on joining us. Although mother had now fully recovered her composure, her relief was palpable when Arthur had asked father's permission to ride with us at the rear of the party.

The beautiful, softly warm day echoed my feeling of contentment as we rode. I was very aware of Arthur's change of mood as he glanced over at me frequently during the journey. I couldn't have been happier.

Word of our arrival had preceded us, and the whole household was at the door. I think that news of Arthur's bravery had spread so quickly through the house that everyone seemed to know of it before we had even reached London. Such is the nature of the gossip grapevine that some is good, some not so good. Mother, in particular, was delighted to be on our own estate once more. At dinner that evening, she was, again, mistress of her own household - confident, relaxed and happy.

"My dear Arthur, I see that you are becoming quite a Gentleman. I have spoken to my husband as I think that should be recognised, not only within this household but in others in the county. Word has already spread of your good ability in reading, writing and arithmetic and I have heard tell of other households wanting you to work for the Lord of the Manor. So I have suggested to your master that you are bought the fine clothing of a

Gentleman, to be worn, of course, when you are not in service to him, but in your own, free time."

Much as I have always loved Arthur's smile, I thought the one he now gave could not have been wider, his pleasure was so apparent.

"I'm indeed very grateful to Master, to you, your Ladyship as well as to Mistress Margory. I'm continuing to learn a great deal from all of you and for that I thank you from the bottom of my heart. I'm not only enjoying reading – although, as Mistress knows, I still struggle with the meaning of longer words – but I particularly enjoy the figures of arithmetic. I'm even enjoying the new numerals that are gradually replacing the Roman. Also, Master is asking me to help with the household accounts increasingly now, and I enjoy doing that very much. I think that is where my skills lie, rather than in book reading. However, I do, of course, enjoy listening to Mistress Margory reading and look forward to doing so for much longer."

"And so you shall", I replied. "Now, as it is only three days to your parents' celebration, father tells me that he has released you from your duties so that you can help them with the arrangements. In turn, you will be pleased to hear that I am also releasing you from reading and writing until two days following the festivities. Of course, your arithmetic lessons will also stop for the moment, but perhaps you can help your father with the bills that he must be receiving connected to the party. There will be time enough for you to be measured for new clothes once the anniversary celebrations are over."

"I hadn't given that a thought, Mistress Margory, but you're right. Father does not enjoy dealing with the household bills and, although my mother is very good at doing them, she never has enough time. Thank you very much. You are all so good and kind to me, I don't know how to thank you. But thank you I do."

* * *

Dear Diary,

Although Arthur is only a short distance from The Manor, at his parents' dwelling, I'm beginning to miss him already. I miss his smiling face at meal and dinner. In particular, I find it very difficult to be without his company in the library each afternoon. It is so very pleasant to have him near me, trying very hard to read in order to please me. His enthusiasm knows no bounds when we turn to arithmetic which he is learning very quickly indeed. Father has told me that he is beginning to rely on Arthur's help with the household accounts so much that he rarely looks at them himself now. I just don't know how we managed without Arthur and I can't imagine daily life without him.

Chapter 66

The day of Arthur's parents' 25th wedding anniversary dawned bright and clear, as though even the weather and the skies wanted to do their best to make the day as beautiful as possible.

Master and Goodwife Wright had invited all the other tenants from father's land as well as some of their friends from the local village of Greenwillows. What I didn't want to do was embarrass the other guests by putting on one of my silk gowns, so I asked mother's advice,

"Mother, sometimes I do wish I had gowns like the villagers' that lace at the front. I'd have so much more freedom to run and dance like they do. Some are even without sleeves, which would be wonderful."

But mother was realistic, if nothing else.

"My darling daughter. It isn't necessary for you to have lacing at the front because you have maids to lace your gowns at the back. The women in the village don't."

"Yes, but I can barely breathe sometimes and..."

"This is all part of being a Lady, my dear. However, on this occasion, ask Ruth to lace the bodice a little more loosely. But just this once."

I finally decided on a pale blue silk and a fairly modestly hooped farthingale. I then directed Ruth to stop lacing the back of it just before it restrained my breathing. This was not quite so flattering as when tightly laced so that my small waist was emphasised, but I intended to enjoy myself at this party. All the servants who could be spared from The Manor had also been invited, leaving some to prepare the food and to help with mother's dressing. Cook, for one, was no longer young, had not danced for a long time and was very happy to be asked to remain at The Manor.

That evening was one of the best I'd spent in my entire life. My present to Arthur's parents was not only the pomanders, but several pewter serving dishes which I gave them before the celebration so that they could use them that afternoon. Wooden tables had been brought in from other tenants and placed end to end to hold the special white breads, meats, home-made cheeses and butter, game pies, salted meats, pickles, preserved vegetables, fruits and candied sweetmeats. There were barrels of ale, and my parents had given several dozen bottles of wine as well as half a dozen hogs to be roasted. Chickens and ducks that were usually saved for their precious eggs were turning and dripping on spits, and rabbits and capons were brought from several ovens throughout the festivities. As I walked the length of father's fields, I inhaled these delicious smells on the unseasonably warm breeze. I felt very relaxed and happy – not least because my looser clothing allowed me to breathe comfortably! Sometimes I envied the villagers who went about their daily lives without the constraints of the wealthy. I knew I was going to enjoy myself.

As soon as I reached the party, I sought out Arthur's parents. Giving them a kiss, I said,

"Many congratulations on your 25 years of married life. I know my mother has also given you my parents' very good wishes."

In spite of Goodwife Wright's warning to me many

years before, when I was too young to understand the word "infidelity", they both looked very happy, surrounded by their children. Someone called out,

"Come and join in the singing, Mistress Margory. We've heard tell that you have a very sweet voice. Would you sing for us on this special occasion?"

"Of course she will."

The appearance of Arthur made my heart soar like the larks overhead. When he took my hand and led me into the centre of the crowd of people, I thought I must be the luckiest woman alive. Then, showing an authority I wasn't used to hearing, he said,

"Before we start the dancing, Mistress Margory is going to sing and the fiddlers will accompany her."

I sang the first song – As I Walked Forth - on my own and received a great deal of clapping at the close. Everyone joined in the next few songs before starting to enjoy the wonderful food. I thought that I must remember to tell cook all about it at The Manor as she would be delighted to hear that such a glorious spread of mouth-watering delicacies had been offered. I was delighted to see that everyone was enjoying themselves. For my part, I thought this was the very best party I had ever experienced.

Eventually, the fiddlers turned to dance tunes which brought almost all to their feet, with a whoop. Then, I couldn't contain my delight at being pulled into the middle of the dancing by Arthur. To add to my pleasure, he showed himself to be a very good dancer. As dancing gave me a freedom I relished, we danced as though we had danced together forever. I loved it. My joy was felt by everyone else who gradually stopped, encircling Arthur and me to watch and clap. But before I knew what was happening, Arthur was leaving the circle and was dancing towards the woods, holding my hand tightly.

My skin began to tingle as our pace slowed and the woods became a little darker. This was where I loved to be, with the earth beneath my feet and my friends, the trees, overhead and surrounding us. It was perfect. Neither of us spoke and Arthur squeezed my hand occasionally, glancing at me to make sure that I was still smiling. I was. Eventually we came to my very own part of the woods that I used to frequent as a child, the area where the sky could only just be seen peeping through the tall trees and the ground was softly mossy. As we both sat down, Arthur touched my face gently, still not saying a word. He looked directly into my eyes which returned his gaze with such love I thought my heart would burst. In his other hand, I now realised, he had been carefully carrying two of my favourite juicy plums. He placed one between my lips, half of it remaining outside my mouth.

"As you seemed to enjoy plums so much, in London, I have brought these especially for your lips only. Perhaps we can share them here."

He then moved towards me and began to tenderly eat the other half of the plum; when the stone was reached, he removed it so that his lips were against mine. He moved his mouth slowly to capture mine and I began to float, as though carried on a cloud. He licked the plum juices from my lips and put the second one in my mouth in the same way. Oh why had he only brought two as I wanted this to never end! This time, as he moved in to suck and eat the plum, his hands gently began to unlace my bodice, at the same time tracing the plum's juices with his tongue down my chin, my neck and to the top of my swelling breasts. Still he was loosening my bodice so that my plump, firm bosom became totally exposed to the fresh evening air of the woods. All the while, his tongue was softly encircling my nipples. I began to take my lead from him by loosening, first his jerkin, then his doublet, caressing his strongly hirsute chest and letting my fingers flow naturally to his swelling manhood. I was surprised and delighted by its strength and size; it seemed the more I caressed it, the harder and larger it became, until I was sure it would spring free of his hose. When I began to feel that I could lose myself totally to these exquisite feelings that were transporting me to another place, a voice was heard, seemingly from somewhere far away.

"Mistress Margory and Arthur. We're missing you at our celebrations. Won't you give us another song, Mistress?"

It took a few moments for both of us to realise that this was Arthur's mother. She must have seen us leave the party, noticed where we were heading and why. I could see that Arthur's face was fuelled with frustration as our journey into paradise had been curtailed so abruptly. Turning away a little, I began to re-lace my bodice – something I was not in the habit of doing myself so was executing rather slowly and clumsily – and to regain my composure. Glancing quickly at Arthur's red face, I felt the full force of his annoyance.

"Yes, mother. We shall be rejoining the party in a few minutes."

His voice was surprisingly cold.

"Good. Then I shall wait for you here until you're ready to accompany me back to our friends".

Arthur's annoyance was equalled by his mother's determination. She stood her ground, turning her head away in order to save me more embarrassment. I stood and brushed down my gown. It was clear that Arthur's and my intimacy was at an end. Gradually, my tinglings were fading, so as graciously as I could, I replied,

"I shall be happy to give another song, Goodwife Wright."

As I began to feel the sensible, solid earth beneath my feet once more, I realised that Arthur's mother had been quite right in bidding our return to the celebrations. A few more minutes and a wild storm wouldn't have been able to interrupt the sea of feelings that were coursing through our bodies. However, as Arthur marched off to join his mother, leaving me to compose myself, I heard strands of "...one of your own kind" and "what would the Master and Mistress have said". The first I cared not a jot about. However, she was quite right about the latter – except that I could have told her word for word what mother would have said – and it would not have been pleasant.

The festivities carried on, I understood, well into the night and, judging by the shadow-eyed servants the following morning, there hadn't been much sleep. Arthur walked back with me to The Manor, neither of us speaking a word. However, what I did realise was that Arthur and I should be married and the sooner, the better. All I had to do now was to make my parents, mother in particular, see the sense of it.

Chapter 67

Little was said the following morning as my parents and I broke our fast, mother and father thinking that I had had a late night and was tired. In fact, my thoughts were quietly occupied with the business of what my next step would be. I wasn't expecting it to be an easy one.

Arthur and I resumed our pattern of classes and, when I heard his knock that first day following our exciting time in the woods, I was ready. In case any tittle-tattle had reached our own servants, I drew Arthur to sit by my side as usual, although not too close, my books and notes laid out before me. Should we be disturbed, no one would know that the subject we were discussing bore no relationship whatsoever to reading, writing or arithmetic.

"You do realise, dear Arthur, that, in the eyes of the church we came close to committing a sin yesterday, don't you, so that must never happen again. Unless, of course, we have been churched. As it is, we are not even betrothed."

My mention of sin brought to mind Hannah's mentioning of it, but I dismissed the thought. She was, after all, ill at the time and couldn't be held accountable for what she'd said.

I allowed my remark regarding marriage to settle for a moment in Arthur's mind. I could see, disappointingly, that this was perhaps a new idea, reflected in his quick, surprised glance at me.

"I want you to know that I have come to care for you deeply, and the affection I have for you is something

I have felt for no other man. I have, of course, experienced strong love for my parents as, no doubt, have you, for yours. But you have made me realise that the love I have for you is entirely different and its expression is totally new to me. No doubt you have had dalliances and, although I do not wish to know of them, I'm glad of it. For I know nothing of these things and would only wish you to guide me down that path, the gate to which we began to open in the woods."

Still, Arthur said nothing and I knew not what thoughts were turning over in his mind. His face had become a blank canvas.

"I wouldn't want you to think, as perhaps your mother does, that it would be impossible for us to be churched. You have now shared my family's meal table for some time. Father is very happy indeed with the work that you do for him, your skill in reading, writing and arithmetic is growing daily and will soon be equal to any of the Gentry in the county. You have shown yourself to be very brave and fully able to protect me, should the need arise. I care not at all that you and your family have no wealth to bring to our coupling. I have all we could desire. I would even consider living with you in one of father's cottages, once we are married. However, I suspect he would not allow that and, indeed, it would not be necessary. I think, too, that he would not insist on your completing your apprenticeship to him, as this would not be appropriate for his son-in-law.

I tell you this to show the extent of my affection for you. What do you have to say? Do you have feelings for me, too? If so, pray do let me know. Do you have feelings for anyone else?"

Father had once told me that it is never wise to ask a question if there is only one answer one wishes to hear. I did notice that, on asking Arthur if there was anyone else, he had looked at me swiftly, his eyes engaging with mine momentarily before looking away. He then said,

"I do need to think about this, Mistress – er – Margory - as I hadn't realised your feelings were so advanced. Nor that you had thought our churching was a possibility."

Noticing that he had only addressed part of my question, I nevertheless brushed that omission aside for the moment. However, it did concern me.

"But what is there to consider? I love you and you love me. That is all that is needed. However, I understand that this would be a big social step for both of us and one that would not be acceptable in some of the county's households. But I care not. Love is the most important thing in this world. Don't you agree?"

"Well, perhaps. Although, I regard ownership of land as important, too."

Racing on, he added,

"Just as your parents will need to adjust to this idea, my own will, too, particularly mother. I shall need to persuade her that it is a sensible step, as well as one undertaken in love."

That was Arthur's first mention of love, but I was sure it would not be his last. I told him,

"Father will think that you are engaged in your studies at the moment, so he will not need your services for some time. Go to your mother immediately and say what needs to be said. She's a good woman and I'm sure she won't stand in our way."

Arthur stood and, straightening to his full, tall height, he lifted his chin proudly.

"Margory, my dear, you will need to learn not to give me orders. While this has been understandable in the past, if our futures are to change in the way you suggest, you must treat me as you treat other Gentry. I shall not be commanded by any woman, not even my mother. My father is not one for giving advice, but he told me only the other day of a book, written about 11 years ago which says that 'women and horses must be well governed'. Also, on no account are you ever to summon me by your whistle, as has happened on one occasion."

This little speech surprised me for I had not realised that I "commanded" Arthur or gave him "orders." But I knew that if he thought so, then I must take care not to do it.

When Arthur had left, I sat a while in contemplation. Arthur was right. This was not, perhaps, going to be as easy as I had thought. But I knew that love conquered all. Didn't it? I did wonder why he had not commented on whether he cared for someone else now, but perhaps I was reading too much into his words, or lack of them. My love would overcome any doubts Arthur had, if he did, indeed, have doubts. As always, it was father I would speak to first, for he would know how best to break this news to mother who, I felt sure, would certainly not be convinced that love was all that was to be considered here.

* * *

Dear Diary,

I told father of Arthur's and my discussion, and I think that he's quietly delighted. As he and mother have not been fortunate enough to have a son - something about which father speaks little but I know is always on his mind, particularly as he grows older - he is more than happy to accept Arthur, of whom he is now quite fond. More than that, he respects his ability to learn quickly and recognises that his gradual acceptance into our society will take place, particularly with his own, strong support. Additionally, Arthur's behaviour in defending us so mightily on the journey into London was very impressive and father lost no time in letting his own friends and colleagues know that. Father was wise enough to recognise that, when fine clothes are worn, people's attitudes immediately change, such is the superficiality of mankind.

Chapter 68

Mother was not happy. Having broken our fast the next morning, she drew me aside into one of the withdrawing rooms on the pretext of our continuing with our tapestries. I was not deceived. Mother is nothing if not plain speaking.

"I'm sure you know, Margory, that your happiness is of great importance to me. So it was with great disappointment and, indeed, concern that I heard your news. While your father is impressed by Arthur's growth in many areas of his work, the fact is, Arthur is a servant. Not only that. He is lowly born, whereas you are high-born. I think it is my duty, therefore, dear daughter, to tell you that I feel strongly that no good can come from this union. That is all I shall say."

I knew that mother and I would never agree on the subject, so, walking over to her, I kissed her warmly,

"Dear mother. I do hope that time will show that love is all that is needed here. All I can hope is that when you see how happy I am, you will be content. I shall, after all, need your wisdom and experience in the coming months, particularly in the arranging of our marriage, which I would like to be soon."

Mother was aware of the importance of an early marriage. Queen Mary's health was failing fast and it was widely thought that Elizabeth would be her successor. That would eventually mean a return to the Protestant faith. That, in turn, meant that our wedding should be conducted as quickly as possible so that it would be in the Roman Catholic way, in which my parents, grandparents and I had been born and raised. However, my mother had another, more immediate concern. Practical, as always, she asked,

"How will Arthur be able to buy the gimmal rings? I really do insist, Margory, that they are made of gold. Otherwise, what would the county's gentry think?"

Personally, I would not have cared if these two hoops were made of reeds. However, mother insisted that we should conduct ourselves correctly from the outset and that nothing but gold would do. I knew that I had to be careful about Arthur's manly pride in this matter, so I suggested to mother that this should be his decision. So when father said that he and Arthur would be travelling North for a few days and Arthur returned with two gold rings, one to be worn by me and one by him, until the wedding ceremony, when I would wear both, I did not question this further.

Chapter 69

As the days progressed, I noticed a difference in Arthur. His face developed a greater determination, his gait became more relaxed and, when he was standing by me, he seemed even taller than before. I loved that. But when he smiled at me and took my arm tenderly while we walked, he was just the same Arthur I knew and had grown to love with all my heart. And now we were joined by the gold rings, too. I knew not how that had happened but it added to my happiness. The betrothal contracts were drawn up by father and Arthur and, again, I did not enquire as to the detail. These were decisions for men to make.

One thing I still hadn't done and needed to do was speak to Goodwife Wright. I was actually far more concerned about her reaction to our plans than my own mother's.

When I arrived at the cottage, she was as hospitable as always and, I noticed, perhaps not quite so humble as in the past. I had always liked and respected her and found her quiet ways endearing. She always made me feel that I could turn to her for sensible advice about almost anything, really, and would always be given something to think on, as a dog gnaws a bone. On this occasion, while we both sat by the hearth with a small ale, she told me,

"I think you know, Mistress, that I don't hold with the mixing of social classes, as I feel it can only end in tears. However, I know how much you love my son. He has changed in many ways, too, during the time he has been in attendance on the Master. So, I hope and pray that everything will work out well and that you will be blessed with much love as well as a large family."

She told me that she would pray for us every day and that was all I could ask of her. This was an honest woman who I would always be happy to help in any way and she would do all she could for me, should I ask. When I left the cottage, I felt the bond between Arthur's mother and me had been strengthened immeasurably and I was glad of it.

Chapter 70

As soon as Arthur and I were betrothed, father had brought up the subject of where we would be living, once married. Arthur didn't have a manor house of his own, of course, so father had suggested that the South wing of the house, which was rarely used, should be renovated to our wishes. Although it only had four bedrooms, two withdrawing rooms, a dining room and fairly small kitchen, father had suggested that it would suit our purposes well until we had a family, at which time he would build a manor house for us on his land. I thought this was perfect, although Arthur didn't seem to quite agree,

"That is very generous of you, Sir. However, I think that, in the absence of our own manor house, I would like the South Wing to be modified so that we have our own entrance. At the moment, of course, the South Wing will require our entry through your own great door and our daily lives will be threaded with yours in a way that I would prefer not to happen, with all due respect. I would like my wife and I to have the independence of our own married life and the privacy of our own dwelling, with its own drive and entrance so that we may enter and leave as well as entertain, without being concerned that we are disturbing your own household. I trust, too, that the windows will be re-glazed during these renovations. I would particularly like arriving guests to see the glitter of glass."

Father had said that may well be possible as he had contacts in London with, not only the Worshipful

Company of Carpenters but also the Guild of Glaziers. He went on to say that he would consider this with mother as he did want our married life to be as we wished it to be. During this exchange, and although, for me, Arthur could do no wrong, I did wonder a little at the extra expense, and hoped that it did not show early signs of greed. But I quickly dismissed the thought.

On our betrothal, father had also told Arthur that he was to be Manager of his estate, in charge of the barns, labourers and stable hands. In that position, he ran the house in conjunction with our head housekeeper. We were, of course, to have our own domestic staff in the South Wing and I was perfectly happy with this arrangement. But perhaps Arthur was right. We would need to have our own privacy.

My own, dear father was so delighted to have a son-in-law he liked, respected and was fond of, that he was happy to acquiesce to almost anything at that time. He spent an increasing amount of time in London which meant that his mind was also, of course, otherwise occupied.

Chapter 71

Work on The South Wing began almost immediately, and we appointed all the staff we needed, from cooks, general servants, to butlers, maids and our own head maid and butler. Once more, I ensured that our female servants were neither too young, nor too pretty. There was, after all, nothing I could do about my own appearance, however much Arthur told me that my eyes reminded him of a beautiful bird's. Although blushing at the time, I was fully aware of my own shortcomings and of the fact that I was envied by more than one young lady in the county as well as all the female servants at The Manor for securing the attentions of such a handsome man. It had not gone unnoticed in the county that he was a rising young Gentleman whose hawking and hunting skills were the equal of any of the other Gentry. I had noticed, too, that his confidence was growing, so I had kept in mind his words regarding my commanding demeanour. At the same time, there was a part of me that could not ignore his servant status. Surely he realised that society had several levels and that my own was higher than he could ever attain.

Chapter 72

Saturday, May 1st, 1557

It was a bright, shiny day that greeted Arthur's and my wedding day. We were married at St Giles church in Greenwillows, our banns having been read before the congregation. Arthur and I had sat through these three readings, during which it was asked, of course, whether anyone knew of any reason why we should not be married. Arthur was particularly restless at these times, but, putting it down to nervousness, I reached for his hand and gave it a squeeze.

"Arthur, my love, why do you seem a little nervous? We both want everyone to know of our love, don't we?"

His answer, "Of course" was a little shorter than I would have liked, but I quickly forgot about it. After all, it was inconceivable that there was a previous marriage or a promise to marry anyone else. He was probably just suffering from a little anxiety at the prospect of such a big event, to which so many would be invited. We just didn't need all this procrastination, nor confirmation of our utter commitment to each other – I knew I certainly didn't. I was delighted that every single person in the county knew of our being united – and here they were, to wish us well.

As I walked into the church with my father, I shivered in the heat as a sudden gust of wind whistled through my hair. I hoped it wasn't a sign of the 'flu epidemic that had killed thousands of our countrymen. A moment later, that thought was swept away by the great oaks, limes and sycamores as they began to sway towards me in friendship and I thought I heard the word "Beware" spoken softly. Of course, it was my imagination playing games as, glancing towards father nervously, he smiled back, giving my hand a pat. The brief change in weather and warning seemed to have been heard by me alone. I told myself it mattered not, for the seasons of late had been inconstant, with great rains, heat and south winds. Nothing was amiss. The bells rang out as though to confirm our love.

"You look beautiful, my dear." said my dear father "Your jewel-covered dress with its gold thread is particularly pretty."

Yes, it was just my imagination playing tricks. As we walked into the church, I glanced to my left, to the font. Hope sprang in my heart that I would be using that often for the baptism of our children. Fairly quickly, we turned right into the aisle of this church that I had known since childhood; I smiled at the multitude of friends gathered to wish us well who were about to witness the hand-fasting. This was to be no hasty coming together, presided over by a man of the church who happened to be there at the time. Arthur and I would be together forever, I knew it. I couldn't wait to say "I do" when our marriage contract would come into being and I would be given the certificate of the ceremony to store safely. Only my dear Arthur would know where it would be.

During that day, the Gentry from the great manor houses throughout Hertfordshire were invited to our lavish feast which was due to continue for two more days. Later, not only were the tenants invited on to our estate for further celebrations, but all the nearby villagers of Greenwillows, too. It was truly a day to remember and I had never been happier.

There was a moment, when we were bidding farewell to the guests on that first day and before I was about to change from my beautiful dress, when I looked everywhere for Arthur, so he could be by my side in saying our farewells and thanks, but he was not to be found. Turning to mother, I asked,

"Mother, have you seen Arthur?"

"No, my dear, not for some time."

Just as I was beginning to worry a little, I saw him,

"Oh, there he is."

Running to him, I took his arm,

"Darling Arthur, I've missed you."

"And I've missed you too, my dear."

As he wasn't looking at me when he spoke, I couldn't quite hear him properly, but he then turned and smiled. Suddenly everything was just as it should be. How foolish I was to have worried at all. He then surprised me by saying,

"I'm sorry to say, my dearest, that I've been called away for the next two days so I won't be able to join the continuing celebrations, much as I would like to."

I was so surprised that I couldn't speak for a moment."

"But..."

Then, turning to face me, he put a finger over my

mouth, saying,

"I shall be back before you know it."

My heart leapt at his touch, as always, and went a little way to still my wondering. So, although I longed to know where my new husband would be and what he would be doing, I did not wish to upset him so early in our marriage, and be accused of commanding him again. So I remained silent.

Chapter 73

While I'd been planning and building my future, I'd been unaware of there being an outside world. After all, what could it have to do with me and my life? I'd noticed some papers father left in the library, but they didn't interest me particularly.

I was only seven years old when Henry's only son, King Edward, and his advisors had introduced Protestantism. Lady Jane Grey's short reign had meant that my Confirmation, when I was 13, had been conducted in Catholicism under Queen Mary. So the country's religious wriggling had hardly affected me at all. I had been married some eighteen months before that grey, November day in 1558 at Hatfield when Elizabeth was told she was Queen and had brought her Protestantism to the throne. Although these were turbulent times, father had tried and succeeded in ensuring that I was shielded as much as possible.

Besides, our lives were full. I now had my own household to manage, albeit a fairly small one. Also, Arthur's management duties meant that, while we broke our fast together, I rarely saw him again until early evening, when he would bound in, give me a perfunctory kiss on the cheek, leap up our staircase, three at a time, bathe and come down to his waiting claret, the glasses of which were becoming more numerous, I noticed. We would then be seated and begin the meal that I had painstakingly discussed with cook.

"Not venison again, Margory! I do declare that your imagination must run dry when you are seated with cook to discuss the menus for the forthcoming week. Perhaps our new pastry cook provides you with a delicacy on these occasions. Your burgeoning body is telling me that you are, once again, enjoying too many sweetmeats. What a pity that the swell does not tell of a happy event in nine months' time. Perhaps your maid needs to be instructed to lace your bodice a little less tightly!"

This was not the first time that Arthur had alluded to my lack of being with child and his words bit painfully.

"I'm sure it will not be long until that happy day dawns", I said softly, but suddenly my appetite was lost.

"I've invited mother to join us this evening. I would like to hear of father's political discussions and to know what's happening with regard to the monarch. Would you like to join us?"

"No. I shall leave you two women to talk and I shall take another bottle of this fine claret to my study."

I was, in fact, pleased to hear that I would have mother to myself as I wished to take her advice on a personal matter. I rarely saw my parents now and missed them very much. I also missed the talk of books. While Arthur was now a very good reader, his real interest lay in accounts and figures, a subject that I had no interest in whatsoever. When my father had suggested that we live in the South Wing, he had made it clear to Arthur that he would be totally responsible for the financial management of our home as well as dealing with the accounts of the estate in general. This was something that I left to Arthur entirely, bowing to his expertise in such matters.

I saw little of him during the early days of our marriage. In fact, I sometimes felt so very lonely that I would join mother and father for their meals, although I preferred not to do that very often as I didn't want them to think that there was something amiss. And, indeed, surely there was nothing wrong? Had Arthur's return at the end of the day been at a reliable time, I would have dearly liked to arrange dinner parties for our neighbours, as had my parents. These gatherings were delightful, as, in addition to my mother's being able to show pride in her kitchen, the meal was usually followed by chamber music or card games. As it was, since my marriage to Arthur, I managed the household, he managed its accounts and we didn't entertain at all. This sometimes made me wonder why Arthur had requested that we had a separate entrance, but I didn't ask about this in case it tempted his fury. It seemed I would have to be content with speaking to my housekeeper and cook every day, as well as continuing with my tapestries, sewing and reading. And, of course, I continued to help mother with her midwifery and was dealing with more deliveries on my own than I had before. Seeing these wonderful miracles of birth and holding the tiny babies made me even more aware and increasingly sad that Arthur and I had none yet. But I was sure that would change and I hoped it would be soon. I tried hard not to dwell on it.

Chapter 74

Shortly after our marriage, I said to Arthur,

"Darling husband. Do tell me what you have been doing today so that I may share in it with you. Now that we are husband and wife, I yearn to know a little more of your life, as, indeed, perhaps you wish to know about mine." However, his reply was given curtly and quickly.

"Wife. I have so much to do each day that I do not wish to experience it again by repeating it to you, a mere woman. You know nothing, after all, of the work of men, just as I know nothing, and care less, about women's work."

On one occasion, when I had been delighted that we were together at dinner, I was shocked when he angrily told me to stop constantly asking him what he had been doing. He had picked up yet another bottle of our best claret and stormed into his study, banging the door. How things were beginning to change – and I didn't understand why. The only time I saw Arthur now was when we were abed, and our coming together was so brief that I had no heart for it. The tender, sensual nature he had shown when we were in the woods was no longer apparent in this newly confident, cold person with whom I shared a bed. What was even more worrying was that there was still no sign of my being with child. This was made even worse one day when he said,

"What's with you, woman? Why are you not yet with child? Maybe you are unable to give me one. The fault certainly does not lie with me."

I looked at him questioningly, wondering how he

could know this. But I thought his statement was probably based on male pride, about which mother had told me a little. So I replied gently,

"Blame cannot be attached to either of us, I'm sure, my dear, and I have not blamed you, Arthur, why would I? I'm sure it is simply that I have not before lain with any man and my body needs to get used to that. While I realise that you have known others physically, like me you have not produced a child either. However, I am sure we shall and I look forward with excitement to that day."

"Yes, well, the tenants' daughters seem to produce children by just kissing a man. Yet here you are, many months into our marriage and still no sign of any fruits of our coupling."

At that, I walked to where he was seated, so very far away from me, and stood behind his chair, caressing his shoulders and running my fingers through his beautiful hair. I loved to show how much I loved him in this way. Gently, I murmured,

"I suggest, dearest, that, when we are abed, you touch me in the gentle, loving way you did when we were in the woods, so that I feel more at ease under the touch of your hands. That experience was so wonderful that simply evoking its memory would, I am sure, lead to a happy conclusion."

At that, Arthur turned to me with such hatred in his eyes that I gasped and stood away from him.

"Let me understand you clearly, wife. Are you suggesting that my embraces do not satisfy you? That my touch does not put you at ease? And that you are, in fact, dissatisfied with our coupling? I cannot believe what I am hearing."

His knife-like words cut through me, and I responded,

"Dear husband, of course, that was not my intention. You are the most handsome, the most attractive and the dearest man I have ever encountered..."

I was speaking to an empty chair. He had thrown down his napkin and, this time, I heard his footsteps running down the steps to the servants' quarters and out of that door. I heard him shout to the nearby stable hand to get his best horse, before galloping away into the night.

That was the first time I had gone to bed alone since our wedding and I sobbed softly, wondering what I had done to turn away a man I loved and who, I had thought, loved me in return.

Chapter 75

Joy of joys! Three months later, my monthly bleeding had not appeared for two consecutive months and I knew I must be with child. Indeed, when I sought out mother and we spoke privately and quietly in one of the withdrawing rooms, her delighted face confirmed that I must be right. I intended to tell Arthur that very evening. So I had spoken to cook the day before about preparing sea bream and instructed the Head Stable Hand to ride post haste to London to buy it. I just hoped that Arthur did not notice that I had given instructions to him; he would not like my over-ruling his authority and I certainly did not wish to annoy him at this wonderful time.

I was in luck, for the stable hand had returned this morning from this secret, sea bream mission and I had rewarded him from my own purse. This wasn't easy, as my husband didn't allow me much money, saying that all I had to do was to ask him.

Arthur was later than usual. The church clock had rung 7 bells, which was when we usually dined, and it was another half hour after that that I heard Arthur's horse. The meal would be a little spoiled, but I didn't intend to allow that to taint my wondrous news.

I ran to meet him in the hall, and, while he was shrugging out of his great coat, I beamed, and gave him a kiss on his dear cheek.

"Have you taken leave of your senses, wife? What ails you? Your place is at table, awaiting your husband."

With that, he gave me a slight push. I don't know

whether it was because our reception hall floor had been newly polished that morning or that I had had to stand on tiptoe and become a little unbalanced in order to reach my husband's cheek, but suddenly I found myself crashing to the floor. Was that moan mine? My husband's height looming over me suddenly seemed sinister as he said,

"Get up, woman, don't just lie there. I need my meal."

With that he began to pull me to my feet. But my legs would not bear my weight and I felt liquid running down them. Surely it couldn't be blood? My thoughts and sight were becoming blurred.

The last thing I seemed to see was Arthur's look of horror as he called for help and several servants came running. I was aware of two of the butlers carrying me up the long staircase and then everything went blank.

Chapter 76

My baby was lost. The surgeon said that, fortunately, my pregnancy was in its early days but that I should rest as much as possible. I was devastated and couldn't stop crying. Just when I thought our baby would bring Arthur's love to me, there was no baby. How could that have happened so quickly?

Arthur had immediately gone to mother who came to my bedside right away, whispering words of comfort while Arthur retired to the study, as usual.

For the next week, mother was at my side as often as her birthings would allow. What irony, I thought, that she must leave the side of her daughter who had lost her child to help others who were producing them. But her words were a comfort to me, at a time when rarely a day passed without tears running down my face.

"You must keep in mind, my dear daughter, that you have shown yourself capable of having a child. The surgeon feels that there will probably be no future difficulties in conception. However, it is very important that you rest and don't become agitated. Your husband, I'm sure, will make certain that you are not disturbed and I shall take over the running of your household until you have recovered fully." In spite of my own, deep sadness, I was nevertheless concerned about my husband, so I asked her,

"While I am abed, would you ask Arthur to join you and father for your meals, particularly dinner, as I would not want him to be alone at this time."

"Why, of course, dear. Don't give it another

thought. I shall suggest to him that he sits with you at the end of his day and then joins us so that he can let us know how you're getting on."

"Thank you, mother."

But my consideration for Arthur was wasted. He neither came to see how I was getting on at the end of each day, nor did he join my parents. He said he was very occupied with his work and didn't want to inconvenience them by being late. I lay reading and praying that all would be well and that Arthur and I would soon be blessed with another child. I had seen so many delightful little ones being born that I longed for one of my own. The sooner I recovered, the quicker I would be able to re-join my husband in our bed. I was sure that everything would be well very soon.

In the meantime, I saw little of Arthur. Just as I was drifting into sleep one evening, I felt a brush of lips on my cheek. Dear Arthur. He must have come to see how I was. But it was father. I tried not to look too disappointed. Gazing at me fondly, he said,

"My dear girl, you have now been apart from your husband for several weeks. Your mother tells me that you have recovered fully yet you remain sleeping alone which may make Arthur feel alienated. I shall instruct the surgeon to make one, final visit to ensure that you have, indeed, recovered. After that, I think that you should re-join Arthur in the bedchamber you share. Your mother can continue to help in the running of your household and, when she feels you are strong enough, you can resume its management yourself. I wanted to pay you a visit before leaving for London, this time for several days. I am very pleased that Arthur now handles my financial affairs for the whole estate, not only the South Wing, so that is one less concern for me."

I nodded sleepily. Father was right. Father was always right. It was not good to be away from Arthur any longer. Why was I delaying resumption of my place in our bed? Also, Arthur had not mentioned his increased financial responsibilities. That must be why I saw so little of him. I thought it was very considerate of him not to mention that to me. Once again, my heart found it easy to soften to him.

That night, I had a strange dream. I was looking down at myself from above the bed, but, although I knew it was me lying there, it was Hannah's face I saw. Hannah who had fallen, just as I had, but in different circumstances. On that occasion, too, I suddenly recalled, I had seen blood on her legs, but had assumed it to be due to the break of her leg. Gazing at Hannah through the haze of the dream, a shock rippled through me as I considered another possibility for that blood. No, that could not be. I dismissed the thought. My dream embodied the guilt I was feeling for my part in her fall. Strange that we had both fallen and that that fall was the cause of so much pain. I wondered if Hannah was looking down on me now, happy to see me confined to bed in the same way that she had been, being advised by the same surgeon and feeling very lonely. I awoke, drenched in sweat, knelt by my bed and prayed. A pang of remorse ran through me. The following day, I would visit Hannah's grave to tell her I was sorry.

Chapter 77

The blue, cloudless sky that greeted me the following morning made me feel very much better. I rang for Ruth who had continued her duties with me following my marriage, and told her to prepare my red dress that suited me so well. By the time mother made her morning visit, I was dressed and didn't intend to delay my return to the household duties any longer.

"I'm so happy to see you looking very well indeed, dear Margory. I shall continue to visit you each afternoon now that you are feeling much better. I shall also help you with the management of your household until you are feeling totally well again. The timing of your return to your husband's bed is, of course, entirely your own decision. All I will say is, it is not wise to be apart from one's husband longer than is necessary."

Mother's words recalled the book to which Arthur had referred when telling me that I was not to command him. It was by a man called Thomas Becon and had said, "...as concerning the bed, married folks may upon due occasion lie the one [apart] from the other, but [it must be] in the good consent of them both...and only for a time, lest the devil be busy." I intended to heed those words.

"Thank you, mother, but I think I'll be able to manage, and shall tell you if I need your help. You've been so kind during my illness but I'm now ready to resume my rightful, wife's place in my home. I shall start straight away by taking a short ride to the church, which will not be too taxing. I would like to thank the Lord for my recovery and it will give me great pleasure to ride Chestnut again."

When I entered the dining room to break my fast, my husband had already left, I was told. Although a little disappointed, I didn't intend to let anything dampen my spirits and, wearing a black woollen cape, I mounted Chestnut astride, a manner that suited my feelings at the time, and set off for the church. This would be a new start. My determination was renewed.

It didn't take long to reach the church and its graveyard and, having secured Chestnut to a tree, I began to wander slowly around, searching for Hannah's name among the servants'. What a sad place this was. So many newborns as well as mothers who had died in childbirth. My heart swelled with pride on seeing that there was only a handful of my mother's deliveries here. The rest were the patients of the other midwives in the area who were not as skilled. I was fortunate that, when my own time for delivery came, mother would be there to help me through it. The surgeon had advised against my becoming with child again for a short while, but I didn't intend to refuse Arthur much longer.

Walking through this melancholy place, my eye was suddenly caught by a well tended area; I walked slowly towards it. How lovely that someone cared enough to keep a grave neat and tidy. It appeared even tidier as it was surrounded by overgrown ones, thick with weeds. On drawing nearer, I saw that there was also a fresh bunch of delicate, wild flowers and that this was, in fact, Hannah's final resting place. I wondered who had left them. Perhaps one of the other servants she had befriended. Perhaps Lucy, wherever she was living. Whoever it was, they must have cared for her very much as it was now some time since her death.

I must have been standing at Hannah's grave longer than I realised. Suddenly, there was a gust of wind and the trees began to sway in exactly the same way that I had experienced on my wedding day. I looked around. The sky was just as clear as it had been. There was no trace of scudding clouds or hint of inclement weather. Again, I thought I heard the wind whispering "Beware". Suddenly, my cloak was almost ripped from my shoulders and I nearly fell. I stifled a scream as I felt a hand on my exposed shoulder. Turning, there was no one there. Rapidly gathering up my cloak, I ran to Chestnut, found a tree stump, mounted and galloped away quickly. Chestnut was delighted to be urged to move with speed, but all I wanted was to be back at The Manor. I wanted to return to the place where I had grown up and where I was welcomed warmly. I had thought that I'd recovered from my accident but I was wrong. My body may be healed but my mind was playing tricks. I'd searched out Hannah's grave with good intent, but found only an atmosphere of malcontent. I was ready to express my sorrow at her death but, it seemed, she was not yet ready to forgive. I did wonder who was remembering her fondly after all this time. I could try and find out by keeping watch, but, for the moment, the graveyard was not a place to which I wished to return. Mother was waiting for me.

"Why, my dear, you look so pale. What ails you? I really did think it was a little early for you to be riding again. Go and rest and I shall come to you later to talk. I shall ask cook to prepare some of her delicious vegetable soup for you. That and our best white bread and you will soon be feeling much better."

"Thank you, mother. Perhaps you're right. I was so looking forward to riding Chestnut again, and he enjoyed it very much, but I don't feel very well and would like to rest awhile. Hot vegetable soup and white bread would, I'm sure, help me to feel much better." Truth be known, I was shaking so much that I doubted any sort of food would help me at the moment. But mother continued her reassurance,

"I shall be back soon, my dear. But first I must see how one of my mothers is getting on; I shall then come to you. Perhaps we could read together."

"I would like that."

Indeed, all I wanted was to feel the calm, comforting presence of my own mother. Although I was 17, I wanted to be treated like a child again. I wanted to be petted and hugged. I wanted to be told that everything was all right, that not only my parents loved me but that I was the dearly beloved of my husband, Arthur, and that he loved me as much as I loved him. I wanted to know that whatever I did was right, that my management of my own household was beyond criticism and that I was the most beautiful woman in Arthur's world. I didn't want to demand his presence. I wanted to know that he couldn't bear to be apart from me for long. I wanted to know that I was the only woman he wished to be with. Above all, please Lord, I wished to lay with him and be with child quickly. Our child. For he was the only man I had ever met whose child I wished to have so desperately.

Just as I thought I was recovering from my loss, I felt close to tears again. Why had I gone to that dreadful graveyard? I'd done nothing wrong. Hannah had died because Lucy had neglected her duties, and that was evident in her running away. I was very busy at the time and couldn't be blamed for any of it. Hannah had slipped on the soap, broken a bone, yet had complained when I was spending time with her, reading to her. I knew of no other lady of a manor house who would have treated a servant in that way. I'd nothing to reproach myself for, had I? I wouldn't visit her grave again. Unless, of course, it was to try to discover who was taking her flowers. I shook myself, as a dog shakes off water. I would return to Arthur fully this very night.

Chapter 78

Later that morning, mother came to see me, just as she had said she would.

"My dear girl, I'm delighted to see how much better you look."

"Yes, mother, I do feel better. I shall instruct cook to serve our meal in the dining room. In the meantime, let us retire to a withdrawing room and talk about what is happening with our Queen Mary."

But our talk soon turned, of course, to events in my own household.

"I do not wish to interfere, my dear, as you and Arthur are only just starting out in your married life. Also, you and he only join us occasionally when, naturally, your father's and Arthur's conversations are about politics and the monarch and our conversation is centred on our own domestic households. I have always known that you are a very capable young woman and I am delighted to see how well you are managing your domestic arrangements. But, of course, our household staff see each other regularly and, servants being servants, they do chatter. Although I discourage this, I cannot eliminate it. At the same time, I do overhear some of it and, while little is of interest to me, I am concerned that there is a subject that seems to be raised on a regular basis. That is, that you appear to take your evening meals on your own quite often and your husband seems to frequent several inns on a regular basis. While you are, of course, aware of dining alone, I am concerned that the reason for this is that Arthur is not engaged in his work for father but seen to be taking a great deal of ale which can lead to other activities."

As always, I felt the pull of loyalty to my husband, as I replied,

"Of course, mother. I know how very hard Arthur works for father, carrying out many and varied duties, all of which father is aware of but I am not. As you know, the position of General Manager is a very responsible one on an estate as large as father's. As a result, I think it's understandable that Arthur is tired at the end of the day and wishes to relax. Of course, I do miss my dear husband's presence at our table sometimes, but I'm proud of the fact that his company is not only sought by Gentry but that he continues to enjoy the friendship of those he grew up with. I think that's perfectly natural for a young man of 16 years old and I'm glad of it."

I wasn't sure whether mother had noticed that I'd talked around her suggestions of "other activities" as this was something of which I was unaware; I would need to think about that. Arthur had a very difficult temper and one that I tried not to arouse. The accident of his pushing me was never far from my mind. I would have to be careful what I said to him. Perhaps I would look into the subject of my chattering household a little more. Arthur and I had only been married for a short time, during which I was trying to organise this, my first household, on my own, without mother's help, and had only been thinking about that. Then, of course, I'd been ill when I'd lost our child, during which I had seen even less of Arthur. I hadn't really noticed whether, and at what time, he'd returned, as I'd withdrawn to a separate bedchamber. However, now I was well again and fully ready to take up my wifely duties in my husband's bed once more. How I longed for our coupling and how I looked forward to holding him in my arms once again. Dear, hard-working Arthur.

Chapter 79

As seven bells chimed that evening, my heart leapt as I heard Arthur's horse. I would exercise the decorum expected of the lady of the household and await his presence in one of the withdrawing rooms with a bottle of his favourite claret.

But my heart was racing and I couldn't restrain myself. My heart full of love, I told him,

"Dearest, how glad I am to have you here with me, and at the time you know pleases me, so that we can sit down together to enjoy our evening meal and discuss the day's events."

Turning his head to avoid my kiss on his cheek, a movement that pained me, he said,

"I shall not be joining you this evening, Margory, and duties on the land may mean that I shall be abed very late. As I don't wish to disturb you, I shall sleep in another bedchamber. So ask a servant to make one ready for me."

"Oh, dearest heart, my bed doesn't gain its warmth until you're resting in it with me. While I was ill, I missed you very much and desire your presence greatly. I'm perfectly happy to await your return to our bed and shall continue to read Utopia until your return. That, of course, will keep me occupied," I added with a smile.

In truth, I didn't wish any of our servants to know that my husband chose to sleep alone, particularly as they knew that I was well again.

At that, I noticed Arthur's neck beginning to suffuse with the red blotchiness that I recognised as the start of his anger; I backed away from him.

"I've told you before, wife, that what I wish in my own household will be what takes place. I've further work to do. I don't know what time that will finish so I shall return to sleep alone. Is that clear? Because if it is not clear, I may repair to my parents' home."

"Oh, please don't give your parents cause for alarm, Arthur. They would think that something is amiss and I wouldn't wish to cause them concern."

"Yes, perhaps you're right. That won't be the place where I shall lay my head this night."

With that, he strode out of the room and to the bedchamber. A short while later I heard his boots in the hall and noticed that he'd changed into his old working clothes. Before I could wonder anew, the door banged and he was riding away. I didn't see him at all that night.

When I knocked on the door of the bedchamber that had been prepared for him early next morning, I saw that the bed hadn't been slept in. I walked into the room and up to the bed. This would not be the subject of more gossip among the servants. Throwing back the linen sheets, I made the bed look untidy, making hollows in the pillows and indentations where my husband would have lain. I then drew back the hangings in the rather haphazard way that my husband used.

While breaking my fast alone, I avoided the sidelong glances of the servants who had provided the usual amount for two of us.

"Don't stare at me like that. What ails you? I've no stomach for food this morning. Take it away immediately."

My irritation was joined by fear as the day wore on. I tried to read, sew and continue with my tapestry but my concentration was lacking. Finally, I decided to ride to church where I would seek some solace in the peace and quiet of the building that had witnessed my move from daughter to wife. I thought I'd been a good daughter, but, it seemed, I needed to learn more about being a good wife. Where was I going wrong? I'd thought that, when I'd learned to run my own household and lain with the man I love, that this would be followed by my bearing children who would be a delight to both of us. With mother's help, I was progressing well, it seemed, with the organisation of my home. However, my husband's love seemed to be disappearing and I didn't know how to re-capture it. Whatever concern I expressed seemed to drive Arthur away a little more; I was at a loss as to what I should do next. And now, he hadn't even come home to his own bed. How had that happened? What could I do about it? I kneeled in church, with tears dampening my face and cloak.

"Please Lord, bring my husband back to me. Restore me to his heart so that we may lie together, lovingly, night after night and that our love will produce a child."

As I mouthed these heartfelt desires, a thought intruded. Had Arthur ever loved me? Had my own desire been so strong, and my heart so full of romance when I saw his handsome face, that I'd failed to see that he may have had other reasons for becoming my wedded husband? Now that he was in a superior position in my father's household, was that all he wanted? Did he gain his happiness by drinking ale and fraternising with his own sort of people? If so, how foolish I'd been to think that reading, writing, arithmetic and learning the manners of the Gentry would enable him to cross the divide of our social backgrounds. Perhaps mother had been right, and my stubbornness had refused to acknowledge the truth. Arthur was, in fact, leading the life he wished, while I was spending an increasing amount of time alone. Had I been blind to what was happening, while even the servants saw and knew that I could not hold my own husband? Idle chatter was alive and well and couldn't be stilled, as I had wished it to be on another occasion. Others saw exactly what was happening for they lived under the same roof as I; what they didn't know or understand, they made up. The result was giggles around corners and whispers behind hands. This was something I had experienced before. Had nothing changed? However much I might try to eradicate such whisperings, I couldn't command its exclusion from the conversation of those whose lives were enriched by it. I must ignore it and try not to add to it.

Chapter 80

I left the church feeling quieter, more composed. The situation with my husband hadn't changed but I felt better able to deal with it. I'd thought to visit the churchyard and Hannah's grave once more, but I changed my mind. I would go and call on Arthur's mother. I'd always liked and respected her opinion, even when it did not, sometimes, concur with my own.

"Why, Mistress Margory, how glad I am to see you. And looking very well indeed. I was so sorry to hear of your accident and illness and hope that you have now recovered fully. I told Arthur that I must walk to The Manor to ask after your health."

My heart leapt. Arthur must, indeed, have slept at his parents' cottage last night! How could I have believed otherwise? Once again, I thought my body would burst for love of him. He'd slept here, at his parents' cottage, so that he wouldn't disturb me. How thoughtful he was and how wrong I'd been to think ill of him.

"So Arthur stayed under your roof last night, did he?"

The words were out before I could stop them chasing across my tongue, so desirous was I to have my worries take to the wind.

Arthur's mother looked at me quickly and questioningly; in that fractured second, I knew that he had not. Her words didn't need to confirm it. For the first time, as she turned away, I felt I was being dismissed. I was the daughter-in-law who couldn't even keep her husband in her bed at night, so what hope was there of a child. In Goodwife Wright's eyes, I was branded. She had, after all, warned me of her concerns regarding our differences in status. And I hadn't forgotten, all those years ago, her mention of the word "infidelity." Was Arthur following in his father's footsteps?

Feeling even more downcast, I said miserably,

"Well, I can see that you have much to do so I shall not detain you any longer."

My pride didn't wish to embarrass Goodwife Wright further and I knew, of old, that she would not honey her tongue with less than the truth.

"I am, indeed, glad to have seen you looking much improved, Mistress Margory, and shall hope that improvement continues."

Yes, Arthur's mother now knew, and this knowledge was not based on tales spread by many mouths but on one, simple question that I had asked.

As I walked outside, I heard the bells chime 10; with each chime the day seemed to grow in length. I realised that I had the entire day ahead of me. How fickle was time. When Arthur and I had talked and laughed together, time had taken wing and passed swiftly. Now that I was alone and despondent, time weighed heavily and moved slowly, leaden-footed. How would I fill my day now that it was becoming clear my husband did not wish to spend evenings in my company? How was my dream of many children to be realised if he preferred the inn to our bed? I didn't have the courage yet to consider where Arthur may be spending his nights. I was not yet strong enough to think on it and would delay its consideration.

As Arthur's sister, Mary, took little George's hand and walked to my horse with me, I glanced at their faces but looked away quickly. I couldn't bear to see again the young Arthur, with his blazing smile.

Chapter 81

That was the first of many days and weeks that were to drag by slowly. I managed the household, I sewed, I read. I didn't seek out my mother's company as oft as I wished, lest that brought questions that I would prefer not to hear. And instead of denouncing the servants' chatter, I strained to hear news, any news, of my husband's activities. My heart stopped its leaping when I heard his horse, followed by his bounding up our staircase and the sounds of his preparing to go out at the end of the day. I no longer planned meals for two with cook, telling her that my husband's responsibilities on the land required increasingly long hours. I told her that, as I did not know when he would be able to eat his evening meal, I preferred not to waste the food that she had prepared so well. Cook knew how much I abhorred waste, lowered her eyes and said nothing.

One morning, mother came to join me to break our fast and I steeled myself for her questions. But it transpired that my own difficulties were not the reason for her visit.

Chapter 82

In spite of my having seen mother only a few days earlier, on looking closely at her face, I was taken aback by its despondency. But my concern was interrupted by her voice that was laden with melancholy.

"Father and I would like you to join us for this evening's meal, Margory. If Arthur is able to come, too, we would urge you to request his presence. We have something to discuss with you, our darling daughter, of a very serious nature. It concerns the unhappiness and confusion that has existed among all our people since the death of our dear monarch, Henry VIII."

My heart lifted a little. It seemed to be only political events that were worrying my mother, so I told her,

"I shall be happy to join you both, mother, as I've missed our talks about political and religious matters and feel that I'm out of touch with what's happening at court."

"Well, that may not be a bad thing", mother said quietly, and smiled wrily.

I was happy to be reverting to my usual course of events in the normal household in which I'd been brought up. First, I asked for my maid, Ruth's opinion on what I should wear.

"Oh Mistress, pardon my asking. Will Master Arthur be joining you then, this evening, for dinner? I'm so pleased."

Her words dampened my spirits for a moment. However, I was not to be turned away from my pleasure of having the good, loving company of my parents again.

"My husband may well be joining us, Ruth, if he can, but I shall, in any case, be dining with my parents in the Great Hall of The Manor."

"Is it a special occasion of some kind, Mistress Margory?"

Although my interest in idle conversation had changed somewhat of late, I would not be the perpetrator yet again.

"I'm very much looking forward to a splendid meal and one at which, I know, there will be interesting discussions."

I liked Ruth and was sorry that I felt the need to avoid her question. However, even I didn't know the real reason for my mother having asked me to join them. So, when I had bathed, perfumed and been dressed in my deep green, silk robe, I made my way to the magnificent hall.

I hadn't seen father for some time and was shocked by his appearance. He was thinner and his shoulders drooped in a way they never had before. His face, also, was clad in sadness and had many more wrinkles than I recalled. He looked much older.

"Are you ill, father? I had no idea and would have come to see you sooner, with your favourite sweetmeats. My own cook is excellent and would be delighted to show her expertise. As you can see, I, myself, am enjoying their sweetness far too much."

"Thank you, my dear, but I'm sorry to say that what concerns me is not to be rectified by sweetmeats, much as I would like that to be the case."

His voice was so sombre that my knife stopped mid-way to my mouth which made a small "o" of surprise. I looked at mother who bade me be patient until father was ready to speak again.

"My dear daughter. You are at the beginning of your married life, whereas your mother and I have now been married, this year, for 24 years, and it has, indeed, been a very happy time. Your mother has managed the household splendidly and has helped our tenants with many medical ills as well as assisting them through the trials of childbirth. For myself, I have been fortunate to have inherited my father's property and have bought further land, all of which has brought forth generous harvests. I thank God for His blessings.

However, England is changing. While our monarch, Henry VIII was deeply religious, even he strayed from Rome, and that created the beginning of great unrest and religious uncertainty. Indeed, just a few years before your birth, the king, while closing the monasteries, faced a threat from devout followers of the faith in the North of England, demanding their re-opening. Again, this led to many executions. Then, his son, Edward, added to that uncertainty, being led by a group of men who took the country down the Protestant path; even puritan John Knox was appointed one of the Royal Chaplains. Then, of course, we had the old faith back, practised under our gracious Queen Mary. As you know, she experienced the sadness of not being with child, as she had hoped, and our true faith died with her. I shall never forget her passing in November 1558 and the funeral procession, a month later, when she was taken from St James's Palace to Westminster Abbey. The following day she was buried with full Roman Catholic rites. By then, of course, Queen Elizabeth was settled securely on the throne.

Daughter, I had hoped that your husband would accompany you this evening, as you will need a protector when your mother and I are no longer here."

At that I lost all appetite and could contain myself no longer.

"While you are not looking well, father, has the surgeon said that you are ill? Why do you speak of taking your protection and that of mother from me? Mother, are you not well either? I'm truly sorry that I've not sought out your company of late. Had I known that you were not well, I would have helped you, wherever I was needed".

Father sighed and leaned back in his chair. I noticed that mother didn't take her eyes from his face for one moment. We waited for him to continue.

"What I have to say is made all the more difficult and surprising for you, my child, because you have been thinking of nothing beyond your own household, and I understand that. However, my journeys to London, through an increasing number of rotting, dismembered bodies – I'm sorry to talk of that before you ladies, but some things have to be said – is stirring up religious fervour all the more. I cannot now have a meeting about the price of ale and bread without someone at the meeting knowing recusants. You will know them, my dear, to be people who, in spite of the monarch's Protestant convictions, continue to worship in the old faith. Some have been heavily fined and some imprisoned. But the numbers are increasing who are tortured, drawn, hung and quartered on the command of Queen Elizabeth".

"Like her parents before her, Elizabeth is well educated, very intelligent and a skilful politician. In spite of being taken to The Tower through Traitors Gate, she emerged, having side-stepped the axe. Her powers of survival are immense".

He paused for breath. I suddenly realised that I had been holding my breath, not knowing where this was leading. After a few moments, father continued,

"We have always been aware that, when she came to the throne on the 17th November 1558 – a date that is emblazoned in my memory - it would, of necessity, be as a Protestant. She had no choice. If she had embraced the old religion she would have been telling England that she is illegitimate, for Henry's parting from Katherine and marriage to Anne, her mother, were not recognised by Rome, as you know. That would have put her accession in jeopardy and she would not have allowed that. She is far too clever. Now that she is on the throne, her main challenge is to remain there.

And now, Margory, it is with great reluctance that I come to the reason for my talking to you about all this. I am well known in Parliament and in local political circles and, of course, my wealth, while having many benefits, also puts me in a position of power and prominence. Because of that, my actions are watched and scrutinised. It is well known under which religious roof your mother and I worship the Lord. I do, of course, conduct myself discreetly on these occasions. However, I shall not turn against the church into which, not only was I born, but my parents before me. Even family friends are now being appointed to commissions to enquire into the number of recusants, so your mother and I are in increasing danger. Once again, the country is becoming divided. Many wives keep the old faith alive in their own households while their husbands attend the Protestant church. Although I understand why this is happening, neither your mother nor I wish to behave in this way. It is publicly known that we worship in the old faith. That puts us in great danger.

I want you to know that I'm not concerned for my own life but, should my beliefs be put on trial by this Protestant monarch, my dear wife insists that she will not leave my side. If that should happen, I can only hope and pray that you and your husband and, God willing, your children, are left alone to live out your lives in peace."

"Dearest daughter, you must exercise full discretion in your worship. You are, I'm sure, becoming fully aware of tittle-tattle and its ramifications. Some is of no consequence, but some must be recognised for the extreme peril it can engender. Only the other day I was told of a man at whom his own brother pointed as being of the Catholic persuasion, only to be dragged to court and accused of heresy. This man's entrails were removed and burned before his own eyes, before he was partially hung, then quartered. Such an ignominious death is not unusual. But it will surely continue for some time, under Elizabeth, in whose reign convictions are becoming more likely. It is being said that Mary of the Scots will be returning to Scotland in the near future; she will, of course, pose a further threat to Elizabeth. It is unlikely that the hundreds of people who met their maker at the stake under Queen Mary will reduce in number under Elizabeth. Your mother and I expect to be among them."

"Margory. You will need to prepare yourself for our deaths. As it is rare for ladies to suffer the additional horror of nakedness, I shall request one last concession – that we are torched together."

Silence of several minutes fell. Father's words hung in the air like swords that could drop and impale any of us, at any time. No one spoke until, finally, I could contain myself no longer. Father's cautions were clear, but I could not stand by and do nothing, declare nothing. Both my parents were gazing at me so sadly that I couldn't bear the silence to continue. Determination arose in me and, spilling over, I told them,

"If you and mother are to be punished for your beliefs, then so shall I. Please, please, father, do not speak of these things. How would I manage without you and mother? I shall not stand by and do nothing if you are to be sacrificed for the same beliefs as I hold dear."

Father's words were equally determined; this was utter seriousness spoken softly,

"And that is exactly what you must do, dear daughter. Nothing. I could not and shall not live and die with the thought that you will endure the same barbarity as your mother and me. If you insist on following us to the grave before your time, my death and that of your mother will have been in vain. We shall die, if die we do, knowing that you will live on to enjoy the fruits of my land and those of your grandfather. You must promise me, Margory, that you will not declare your religion openly, but will pursue it with discretion and only with those you trust utterly. I cannot go on unless you give me that promise. Until now, it has not been necessary for us to use the chapel I had built in The Manor very often and, indeed, its existence is not known to those outside the family. It is there you must worship. Is that understood, Margory? Utter secrecy will be absolutely essential. Promise me."

What had started out as, I had thought, a pleasing repast, had turned into a meal that perhaps would be one of my parents' last suppers. How could I live without them? How could I live with the knowledge that they were to be put to death? Above all, how could I stand by and see them suffer so much that the thought of it sent me into a paroxysm of fear? I wanted to scream and scream until my throat refused to be the vehicle of such terrible emotion. If only my husband was here so that I could lean on his strong shoulder. How could I endure, how could I live on with this terrible possibility, the picture of which my father had painted as one so horrific I could not begin to contemplate it.

I straightened my back and raised my chin. My husband was not here. He was in my company less and less and his shoulder was no longer one on which I could lean. I must learn to live my life without him, too.

"Promise me, my dear daughter."

Father's quiet voice pierced my thoughts, bringing me back to where I was sitting. I had never before seen my parents' faces so lined with worry, so full of grief. I knew then that I must do exactly as my father wished. I reassured him,

"Dear, dear father. Of course, I promise. Should events take place that you've described as possibilities, and should the unthinkable happen so that you and beloved mother are taken from me, I shall obey your last request. Although I know that I have not always been a dutiful daughter, I hope that I shall be given the strength to fulfil this final request of a father who has been without fault. No man could be better and no man deserves what you may have to suffer. I shall do as you ask and continue to worship in the only true way, but I shall exercise the utmost discretion in doing so. While it breaks my heart to have to exercise my faith in secrecy, if that is necessary, then that is what I shall do. Yes, I promise, dear father."

Chapter 83

July 1561

I'd heard that the Queen was making one of her many progresses, starting by water, leaving by road, with all her trumpeters, heralds, lords and ladies. Everywhere I rode was crowded and, on my return to The Manor, I saw a horrific sight. When nearing the stables, there were a dozen men on horseback, with two figures seated before them. With all eyes on the queen's rich pageantry, no-one would have noticed such a small band, destined for death. Even I wondered if they were part of the queen's pageant – until I went into The Manor where my eyes blurred with tears. Everything had been ransacked, valuable paintings and silverware had been taken and the servants were wandering around in a daze. The housekeeper rushed to me.

"Oh Mistress Margory, thank God you're safe. We thought they'd come for you and Master Arthur, too. They didn't touch the library and the Master said to tell you he's left word in there for you."

Closing the library door softly behind me, I saw the letter I was to cherish always.

"Darling daughter, I have just heard that the queen's men are on their way to arrest your mother and me. I beg you, don't try to see us as they will certainly arrest you, too. Arthur has been totally in charge of the finances of The Manor and my land for some time now, so he will tell you that the two of you have inherited a great

deal and are now extremely wealthy. Treat your inheritance wisely, Margory, for our sake. God willing, you will have a family of your own so that my work and that of your grandfather will not have been in vain and will be continued by your children after you are gone.

Margory, you are now mistress of The Manor and Arthur is its Master. Your mother tells me that you have run your own household well since your marriage, and I'm glad of it. As for Arthur, his skill with figures is excellent so there should be no difficulties there. Your mother also tells me that you and he are having difficulties. While I was very saddened to hear this, it may only be due to the fact that you are in the early stages of your married life together. I do know that you love him and I pray that he loves you equally. I trust in God that He may bring your hearts together and soon so that you will bear several children. When that day dawns, tell them about your mother and me, that we have done no wrong except to worship God under a different roof from that of the monarch. I do not understand why all those who believe in one and the same God cannot be left in peace to worship Him in the way they wish, where they wish. Perhaps, one day, these divisions in the Christian church will be eradicated and all will worship together. What a wonderful thought that is, but how foolish of me to think on't.

Finally, my dear, do not weep too long for your mother and me. We have had good lives, and a long life in each other's company, and we leave this life together. That, at least, is something that pleases both of us greatly. Above all, never, ever forget the promise that you

gave me.
Ever, your loving father."

I moved the letter away so that it did not become drenched in my tears. Of course, I was sure I must be to blame for this. My parents were good people who had never wronged anyone in their entire lives. Whereas I... I had become so intent on having Arthur that I had seen no one and nothing else for several years. And I had ensured that nothing and no one came between us. Mother, in her gentle wisdom, had tried to show me that I was taking the wrong path, and Arthur's mother had been very direct in telling me that my coming together with her son was not the sensible way forward. Then, when I had observed a closeness between Hannah and Arthur, I had tried to ensure that did not continue. Kings and queens had come and gone, bringing their different religions with them. During those times, father had described increasing unrest as the people no longer had the strong beliefs of the old religion to cling on to and acknowledge. But I had only seen blue eyes and a wonderful smile in a handsome face. A face that I rarely saw now. It was time for me to change that. If Arthur would rather lie with someone else, he must acknowledge it. For now, I must get the servants to work putting The Manor to rights; first, though, I would ride to church for the final time and pray for the souls of my mother and father. If I was seen, I would say I was visiting the grave of my maid, Hannah.

My ride on Chestnut was not the joyful flight I usually took and he, sensing my sombre mood, moved slower, as though to protect me. When I dismounted, I stroked his neck and he whinnied softly, acknowledging my distress. Glancing around to ensure that no one was witnessing my entry to the church, I prayed for my parents and also told the Lord that this would be my last visit to His house as I would now be worshipping in private, in my own home. I knew He would understand. On Hannah's grave, there was, once again, a fresh posy of flowers. The grave had also been tidied so that it had the appearance of a small, well-tended garden. I wondered again who this person was who had cared so much for Hannah that they continued to visit her and offer flowers? Surely it couldn't be Lucy, who had last been seen walking away from here and perhaps had decided to return to her place of birth. Although I wondered still, my thoughts were now on much more serious matters.

When I returned to The Manor, in spite of being the embodiment of sadness, I found I had a new resolve. I sat straighter on Chestnut and looked around at my father's beautiful land. Land that I must ensure continued to bear the fruits of my ancestors' labours. I would also start my visits to the tenants once more to continue my mother's work of healing and midwifery. I would certainly ensure that my parents' deaths were not in vain.

Chapter 84

I was surprised to hear Arthur's horse that evening, just as I was preparing to tell cook that there would only be a need for one meal, again. He must have heard the news of my parents and wished to console me. Even then, my heart still found it easy to warm towards my husband. But words of cold steel met my warmth.

"Wealthy? You and I? No. There's no money for us."

"What do you mean there's no money? How can that be? Father and his father before him have acquired a great deal and in father's final letter to me he assured me that you and I have inherited all they have built over the years."

Arthur stared at me condescendingly.

"Wife. You taught me all I know about arithmetic, your father then taught me about finances and, for some time now he has left all financial management to me. I didn't say that we have no wealth, I said that you do not. Oh, you have what was left in the house when your parents were arrested, as well as, of course, the small inheritance left to you alone by your mother, which I could not touch, sadly. But everything else is mine now and I've already enjoyed spending a great deal of it. Remember the house your father spoke of building for us? It is built. But not in Hertfordshire, in another, far-flung part of England where you will never step foot. Its mistress is the mother of my child and a second will soon be bawling. She is young, pretty and used to be a member of your own household, so was worth the risk of a Special Licence. When I built my home there, we were known to no-one anyway and were perfectly happy to dispense with a church service. Oh, she cannot read or write and arithmetic should be left to men anyway, but she warms my bed well. Her father is a farm worker, like my own, and she does not try to command me. She's obedient, does my bidding and is learning to manage our household and its growing number of servants well enough. Do you seriously think that I would have considered marrying you unless you'd been rich? I took a risk in church during the reading of our banns as I was already intimate with my woman. But no-one knew of her existence in these parts."

I stared uncomprehendingly. I could barely believe what I was hearing. How could this be true? All this time, while I knew that all was not as it should be, I had thought, like my parents, that these were the growing pains to be expected when two people were living together for the first time. How could I have been so blind? How could I have been such a fool as to think that my own love for Arthur would conquer all and that all would be well?

Suddenly I found my tongue.

"Divorce is impossible."

"Ay, and so it may be, but a legal separation isn't, although, when I bought the Special Licence, I secured the silence of the Church authority by doubling the 10/- fee. I don't think the man had ever seen such an amount. But if he should speak of it, I shall seek annulment. Is it not enough for you to know that I do not desire you, and never have?"

How easily was forgery bought, I thought.

"Does your mother know any of this?"

I was trying hard to regain some essence of sense.

"No she does not. And if I hear that she has been told, I shall know by whom and you will wish you had remained silent, for I shall not have my mother upset. She never supported our marriage. She is too sensible for that. When my woman has been delivered of our second child, I shall send for my parents to live with us. Lord knows the house is big enough. However, I think it unlikely my mother will agree to that. You and she are a lot alike. She's strong-willed, and so are you. But your difference lies in the fact that she allows my father to go his own way, whereas I would have always been commanded by you. And that I would never have tolerated."

Although almost speechless, I managed to spit out,

"But what will happen to my father's land? It needs to be managed. The labourers need someone in charge of them."

"I care not. I've my own land and plenty of it. For all I care, your crops can rot, for there's no one to take my place. I have ensured, in the time I've been in charge, that all the good workers have left and their replacements prefer their ale to work. Already, the estate is declining, the buildings are falling into disrepair and there is now no money to do anything about it. Oh, this has not happened quickly, but gradually since shortly before our wedding day, at which time your father left all management and financial affairs to me. He increasingly has been concerned with political and religious matters and I've seen him less and less. He trusted me, and that was his mistake."

At those blistering words, I shouted

"Get out! Go to your mistress and your bastards. You took my father's trust and strangled it. You used my love for your own greedy purpose and were never worthy of it. But you shall have it no more. I'm glad that I now see you for the selfish son of your father that you are. My father was a good man who thought you were also someone he could trust to protect and care for me, his only daughter. That he was wrong increases your worthlessness as well as his generosity. He loved you because I loved you and that's an end to it. But listen well, Arthur. By the time I have finished, the whole county of Hertfordshire will know of your behaviour, and if your mother learns of it then, you will not be able to lay blame at my door."

"I think you're forgetting one thing, Margory. You are no longer the wealthy owner of The Manor of Greenwillows. You have nothing. Who will have ears for you now? Your parents have been torched, you couldn't keep your husband happy, you have no children and your father's land and buildings are in need of repair. Yes, I shall go. I care not who knows as I am now a land owner in another county, far away from here, where no one knows that you even exist. I have a loving, pretty woman, children, a grand house and fertile land, while you have nothing. The only reason I've returned here is to ensure that Hannah's grave remains as pretty as she was, as would her child and mine have been".

Chapter 85

That final admission was more than I could bear; I reeled in shock. But I would not give him the pleasure of seeing that he had caused the death of part of my heart. I turned and walked stiffly into the library, closing the door softly behind me. But the sound of his horse galloping off released a stream of tears I thought would flow forever. I sat in my dear father's chair, laid back my head and sobbed for I know not how long. How could my life have changed to such a degree that I no longer recognised it? I couldn't pay the servants or the labourers. My beautiful silk dresses would remain unworn as I would have no reason to wear them nor a maid to help me dress. I had no mother or father. Now, I realised, I had never had a husband either. Not a real one. Not one who took over my protection from my father. Not one who wanted to lay with me so that we would create our own family in the way I had always dreamed. All he wanted was to lie to me, not with me.

I didn't notice when the room grew dark, when the sun slid below the horizon and the stars pricked out their glitter in the sky. Finally, I heard a soft knocking on the door and, with an effort so huge, I dragged myself back into the woken world. I must make my eyes see what they did not want to see. Words must be uttered by my mouth that I had never thought my ears would hear.

"One moment." The two words wobbled.

I swallowed, smoothed my dress and wiped my eyes. This was the first day of the rest of my life and I must live it with dignity. If I had to live it on my own, with God's help, I would do it. First, I must speak to the servants, followed by visiting all the tenants. This was not going to be easy.

The housekeeper, Goodwife Sykes, came in and looked at me in dismay when I told her there was no longer any money.

"How can this be, Mistress? Your good parents not long gone and, suddenly, there's no money to pay us?"

"I would prefer not to go into the details, Goodwife Sykes. Suffice to say, that the person into whose hands father entrusted the financial management of the estate was not, in fact, to be trusted. They have spent it on everyday living as well as building an estate of their own – totally unknown to anyone in this household. I am truly glad that father is no longer here to see how the wealth created by my grandfather and him has been squandered for this person's own gain. I am as shocked as you are. All I can say is that I shall be more than happy to speak or write to any prospective employer for any of you. You have served this household well and I shall not forget that. Until future employment is found, anyone who wishes to do so is more than welcome to remain under this roof. However, as there is now little money, I shall not be able to pay any wages and shall, in fact, have difficulty paying for daily meals. So if anyone wishes to spend this time with their family, I shall not insist on their staying here. My wish is for everyone to be newly employed so that they are able to eat and be clothed.

Now, would you please gather everyone in the Great Hall so that I can speak to them. If, after that, anyone wishes to speak to me individually, I am happy to do so in the library."

No one did. A sadder group of people would have been hard to find. That, and sheer puzzlement stared back at me in disbelief. Some wept, others comforted. This was one of the most difficult tasks I had ever had to undertake in my life. Most of these people standing before me had served my parents faithfully and well for many years; it broke my heart that I was the messenger of such news. One brave soul asked how it had happened that, while my parents lived there had been money a-plenty, so where had it gone.

I didn't intend to tell the county that, not only I, but my father had been taken for fools by a person who was unworthy to step into the shoes of my father. Indeed, whose shoes this person had polished not very long ago. I was still not clear, myself, how this turn of events had happened right under my nose.

But one thing I did know. I would never be duped by a handsome face and dazzling smile again. Arthur's mother's teaching of the word "infidelity" rose like bile to haunt me. If another unfaithful man ever crossed my path, he would wish he had not. That was my promise to myself.

While the servants, in melancholy mood, drifted away, I prepared myself to speak to the tenants. This would include, of course, Arthur's mother, who I would tell no more than anyone else. Indeed, when I told her the news, I knew she was as surprised and shocked as everyone. She was, however, astute enough to realise that Arthur was nowhere to be seen and that asking about his whereabouts would implicate her in the same ignorance that I had experienced. Goodwife Wright was a good woman; she had always made it clear that, in her opinion, Arthur's step up in society was a step too far. However, it was not only one that he had taken, but he had taken it with the full support of me and my father. Although she was his mother, I didn't believe for one moment that she would approve of the way he had gone on to behave, even though she might understand it. So, it was with a heavy heart that I gave her the bare facts in exactly the way I had told the servants. I omitted Arthur's part in it. If she guessed, it would only be a partial truth and she, like everyone else, would never learn of his actions from me. He was, after all, her eldest son.

Chapter 86

That night was the first time in my life I had had to disrobe myself, with no help; I barely knew where to begin. Part-way through, and clad only in my silk chemise, I sat on my bed – the bed that Arthur and I had shared on so few occasions – and wept once more for so long that I thought there would never be an end to it. Then, through my sobbing, I heard a soft knock.

"Who is it?"

"It's Ruth, madam. I thought I heard sounds from your chamber. Can I get something for you?"

"Come in, Ruth, and close the door behind you."

Her face was full of kindness as she addressed me,

"Oh, Mistress Margory, I would have gladly helped you prepare for your bed. Here, let me put away your clothes."

"You do know, Ruth, that I can no longer pay you to help me, don't you? You have been an extremely conscientious maid to me and I do thank you for all the duties you've performed in the past. I'm sure that you'll have no difficulty at all in gaining another position on an estate such as this. Or, I should say, such as this used to be. And I shall be happy indeed to see you settled. As you know, I have let it be known that everyone is more than welcome to stay under this roof until such time as you find alternative employment. However, I'm now not in a position to pay for anyone's labour so I shall totally understand if any of you wish to return to your families. In fact I would encourage you to do that. This house and estate are no longer as happy as they once were, with mother organising everything beautifully before helping the tenants through their illnesses and birthings."

Ruth looked pensive and, when our eyes met, I realised that I had never really looked at her properly before. Although she wasn't a pretty girl, she had an intelligent, very kind face and she was looking at me now with such empathy and consideration, I thought I should start weeping all over again.

"Is there something you're wanting to say to me, Ruth?"

"Begging your pardon, Mistress. I hope you won't think me too bold, but I think that I speak for the whole household when I say that no one has been happy to see you, first become ill and then without the company of your husband. And, of course, at just the time you needed his support when your parents were taken away, he was no longer seen on the estate."

"You are right in saying that you are being very bold, Ruth, and I urge you to take care in what you say."

Although Arthur had broken my heart, the news of his actions was still very raw and I still felt a kind of loyalty to the man I had loved. I was beginning to realise that one of my many faults was misplaced loyalty.

"All I wish to say, Mistress, is that we're happy to stay by your side, giving any help we can until we've found employment elsewhere. We don't wish to see you so alone once more at this very difficult time."

I had never known that such loyalty could exist between servants and their employers. This was all too much to take in. Suddenly, I felt so weary that I lay back on the bed, feeling all strength leaving my body. I shivered. Had Hannah returned to haunt me yet again in my weakest hour?

"Are you well, Mistress? You've become very pale."

"Ruth, your words of comfort have moved me deeply and are more than I could ever have hoped for. I would like to be left alone now. Would you tell housekeeper that I shall speak again to everyone at 9 of the clock in the morning."

"Gladly."

To my amazement, while my eyes were closing, I felt a feather-like brush of her lips on my cheek and she was gone. It took me back to when my father had also kissed me softly on the cheek. A surge of strength flowed through me.

Chapter 87

When the household were all assembled the following morning, I led everyone down to the kitchen, with its very large table, so that they could all be seated. I felt that informality was more appropriate to the present circumstances; I did so want everyone to feel that they could speak to me confidently and in a relaxed fashion. The housekeeper was first to speak.

"Mistress Margory. I know that I speak for the entire household when I say that we deem ourselves fortunate to have served your family. We all respected your parents highly and the manner of their deaths is beyond comment. Suffice to say that we shall never forget their goodness which permeated this estate daily. Some of us have known you since you were born and, if you don't mind my saying, those of us who have had that privilege hold you in deep affection".

I held my breath, not knowing what may come next.

"We also knew Master Arthur, of course, and were delighted to see you so very happy on both your betrothal and wedding days. We fervently hoped that would be the start of another contented household and that you would be blessed with several children. It appears that is not to be, at the moment anyway, and it's important that we value the lives we live today and pray that we shall be spared to live for many years to come.

In the meantime, we burned many candles last night – begging your pardon, Mistress, for their cost – discussing how we can earn money for food and clothing.

What we've decided is this. We shall all turn our hands to any skills we may not have used for some time. Beatrice, your late mother's maidservant is an excellent seamstress, Maud is a talented pastry cook, Thomas, your late father's Groom will offer farrier services. Even Stephen, your late father's retired manservant, who loves gardening, has said that he will take his prize vegetables to market and contribute those earnings. There are still other members of the household – mainly the very young – who are unsure what they can offer, but are willing to learn, according to their interests. However – and again, with your permission – we shall sell our wares from the market stalls of our families. That will require no further financial outlay. We shall then put all those earnings together to buy food and, hopefully, clothes."

I listened, speechless. How could so much goodness have grown under my family's roof and not been abundantly clear to me before? My parents had always been very supportive of my actions and desires – well, almost always – but I'd never considered the possibility of such strength and generosity being found in our servants. But that was my weakness, not theirs. They were, after all, human beings, just as we are. Had I not always enjoyed the company of the tenants, throughout the nine months of the women's carrying their babes? Had I not shared in their joy on the safe deliverance of both the mothers and little ones? And had I not preferred their celebrations, danced with abandon and laughed with them all my life? It had never been for me the stiff awkwardness of formal occasions at The Manor, the dressing in silks and satins. Why had I not recognised this before? Even when all around me were frowning on my choice of husband, I had cared not. My mistake there, of course, was the man, not his social standing. But he must now be as dead to me as my parents. Although my feelings of love for mother and father were still strong and would always remain so, those for Arthur had begun to diminish as his side of our bed grew cold. I was reminded of having heard someone say recently that war and poverty dissolve social boundaries. What a pity it was that these two extremes were required in order to do that.

I realised that I had been standing, saying nothing, for several minutes and, with tears in my eyes, I looked around at the eager faces awaiting my approbation of their suggestions. And so I told them, with a bursting heart,

"Well. I cannot begin to express my gratitude enough to all of you for this wonderful support that fills my heart with joy and humility. During the next few days, I would like to see each of you individually so that we can plan what you'll be doing and how much you're expecting to earn. It's only right and proper that a part of your earnings should be kept aside for your own use entirely. I would like each of you to think about how much you will be willing to share in the buying of food. For my part, I'll continue to minister to the ill among the tenants as well as delivering their babies. I couldn't begin to consider taking payment for that. But perhaps I could offer my services to those further afield and make a charge to them. I think that would be perfectly reasonable, and it's something I shall consider further. There is a great deal to think about and I do have a small amount of money secreted away. So, cook, let you and I put our heads together and arrange a celebratory meal. Not the sort we have been accustomed to here, at The Manor, of course, but a coming together of everyone's favourite food. When I speak to each of you in the next few days, I would like you to tell me what is your one favourite dish, and that will be included in our modest feast. I'll also invite the tenants, once I've spoken to each and every one of them. We'll then decide on a day for this wonderful time of thanksgiving. This will be my thanks to all of you for your past work as well as your present and future comfort and assistance. I cannot find words appropriate enough to thank you all so much. It's something I shall never forget. And now I must go to the library."

I hastened away before emotion overwhelmed me yet again.

Chapter 88

I now closed the library door and slid the bolt softly. Going over to one of the book shelves, I withdrew a book and pressed a button. The whole set of shelves then submitted to being opened, revealing a small door, about four feet at its apex. Although only five feet tall, I had to crouch down low to enter and, on the other side, I could not stand up fully. Not even Arthur knew of this place. In it, for some time, I had been gathering the means by which I could worship in peace and in secret. As I sank to my knees, I thanked the Lord for delivering me safely to this day and for giving me such faithful, loyal servants. No, they had proved themselves to be far more than servants. In these most difficult times, they were fast becoming friends, which was something I could not have envisioned. Kneeling there, with our Lady looking down on me, I felt my troubles begin to melt away. Although I knew not what the future held, I now was certain that, as well as the Lord's guidance in Heaven, I had the support and help of those in my household, here on earth, for which I was truly grateful. I closed my eyes and gave thanks. I felt at peace.

Rising awkwardly, I crouched my way out of the small room and walked back into the library, placing the panel of books back into place and quietly unbolting the door. No one must ever find this sacred place or I would follow in my parents' footsteps. Laws may be passed against the punishment of dissidents, but we all knew that searches continued. Once again, father had been correct in his insistence that I worship in utter secrecy and that is what I intended to continue to do.

There was a knock on the library door and I invited in the first of the servants. This was the start of living my life in a way that I'd never experienced before. I had a great deal to learn and that satisfied me as I'd always enjoyed learning. But this time, there were to be no books or tapestries, but the ordinary, everyday activities such as dressing and bathing myself. Above all, I had to work with cook to ensure that no food was wasted and meals were prepared using only those ingredients that we had the money to buy. These tasks of mine must be threaded between continuing my mother's work of tending the sick among the tenants as well as delivering their babies. If there were any hours remaining in the day, I must go further afield to practise my midwifery and for that work I must take payment. It would be difficult and tiring. However, I now had the increased responsibility of not only managing all the estate – work about which I knew nothing - but ensuring that the help of the devoted people in my household who had shown themselves to be loyal and strong in the face of adversity did not go unrewarded. I must not and would not fail them. However, I'd no idea what I would do about the labourers in the fields who Arthur had described so disparagingly.

Chapter 89

"Mistress Margory?"

I was bumped back from my dream and thoughts of all that had happened before I'd moved to Brockminster. Had I fallen asleep? No, there was Goodwife Sykes, my wonderful housekeeper, with, was it Lucy, standing looking at me enquiringly?

Of course, my land was now in the capable hands of Hugh Taylor, my servants had become good friends, but what of Lucy? Why was she here? If it was her. Why had she run away? Where had she been? All these questions were bouncing around in my head - it all seemed such a long time ago. My life was now unrecognisable compared to that I had led with my dear, late parents at The Manor.

"Is it really you, Lucy? Thank you, Goodwife Sykes. I shall speak to Lucy alone".

"Of course. Just ring if you need anything, Mistress Margory."

"Thank you."

Feeling puzzled, I turned to the young girl standing before me. She was still pretty, but now there seemed to be an air of greater maturity about her that went beyond age.

"Lucy, come and sit by the fire. Tell me. How are you, and what made you run off and leave Hannah? I'm sorry to say that she was very ill when you left – something that none of us realised, except, perhaps you – and died. That was in spite of my family surgeon's care."

"I'm truly sorry, Mistress, that Hannah died. I was

very frightened. Only overnight, she turned from being a friend into someone who didn't recognise me at all. As she was also very hot and sweating, I thought she had a fever that I may be infected by. I'd experienced this on one other occasion. My own, dear mother had taken to her bed and suffered in exactly the same way. I couldn't bring myself to witness that again, Mistress Margory. So I decided to go back to the village of Biggleswade where I was born. However, I hadn't got very far when Master Arthur came galloping up. He asked what I was doing and where I was going. When I told him I was thinking of going back to the village where I was born, he said he had a better idea. He said he knew of a manor house in Bedfordshire, the mistress of which was looking for a Lady's maid. I went to see them with him. He told them that I worked hard and they said they'd give me a trial for 3 months. I was so relieved that I'd found work that I felt very obliged to Master Arthur. I didn't know then that he was doing this for his own, selfish reasons. He continued to visit me there until, one day, he said he wanted to take me to a grand house he'd bought in the north-west part of the country. I didn't know why he was asking me to go there, Mistress Margory. All I knew was that I might be lifted out of my life of poverty which I'd known with my mother and father. When we went there, I couldn't believe how very big it was, and told him that it was far too good for the likes of me. However, he said he wanted me to be its mistress and that we would start a family. Although I'd always liked Master Arthur, I'd never loved him, as I'd only looked at him as your own intended. But he's a very persuasive man, Mistress, and what with the size of the house and the thought of having my own babes, I agreed. Indeed, at the time, I felt very excited, and that my life was changing for the better. But I was wrong.

From the start, he began to stay away a lot until, when I was expecting our second child, he hardly came home at all, saying I was fat and unattractive. It was only then I realised that the only reason he'd asked me to live with him was because I looked like Hannah, and that he'd never loved me at all. He eventually told me that Hannah had always been his first choice and, when she'd fallen, she'd lost their child. I just couldn't believe what I was hearing. At the same time, he said he wasn't interested in someone who limped. That really hurt my feelings. But when I told him the limp seemed to have started when you'd looked at me oddly in the library at The Manor, he suddenly seemed more interested. He asked me for details of exactly what had happened. I don't know why."

"If I've done wrong, Mistress Wright, I'm truly sorry."

I listened to this story quietly, thinking back to the day I'd turned on my mother so unexpectedly, to George Hardcastle's unexpected death as well as to Lucy's limp that had suddenly appeared. Did they all have something in common?

I thought back to the rumours that, on January 30th, 1536, the day after Anne Boleyn's miscarriage, she had previously charmed Henry into marriage using witches' powers. Had my own youthful feelings been so very wilful that, first, I would go to any lengths to make

Arthur my own, including turning on those who appeared to stand in my way? Then, when that passion had turned sour, had I turned it against all unfaithful men? Surely turning on my mother was merely youthful, selfish temper? The cause of George Hardcastle's sudden death would now never be known, of course. And, in my mother's medical ministrations, I'd heard tell of something called arthritis. Could this be what ailed Lucy? Or was I really a witch?

PAMELA MANN

Pamela had her first article published when she was 15 and went on to gain a degree in English Literature. Since then, she has been an editor of corporate magazines as well as fiction books and a writer of articles, press releases, pamphlets, leaflets and websites. She also teaches English and creative writing and is a member of the Historical Novel Society, the Scottish Association of Writers and Verulam Writers.

Pamela's inspiration came from Arthur Miller's The Crucible and her own passion for fairness.

Pamela is a reader at The British Library and The Wellcome Institute in London, England as well as using the expertise of The Royal College of Midwives. One of her primary sources of research has been the first book written by a midwife in 1671. She has read the books of many notable historians, in particular, Dr Ian Mortimer.